RETURN

DRAGONBORN, BOOK TWO

BRETT HUMPHREY

Protect the weak!

BRETT HUMPHREY AUTHOR, LLC

Print ISBN13: 978-1-73411-763-9
eBook ISBN13: 978-1-73411-762-2

This book is a work of fiction. Names, characters and incidents portrayed within its pages are purely fictitious and a product of the author's imagination. Any resemblance to actual persons, living or dead, is purely coincidental.

Published by Brett Humphrey
2487 S. Gilbert Rd.
Ste. 106-105
Gilbert, AZ 85295

To Jennifer, my biggest fan and supporter.
Thank you for being on the adventure with me.

To those who love to read, we can change the world if we choose to
positively impact people we come into
contact with each day.

ACKNOWLEDGMENTS

I wouldn't have made it this far in my life and my new endeavor as an author without the following influences:

Jennifer, Kenny, Sarah, Josh, Chelsea, Sofie and Avery, you are an awesome family and have never complained when I headed to my desk to write every night!

Cyndi and Erich, thank you for being an amazing sister and brother. You have always supported my creativity and you cheer me on.

Dana, Kira, Anthony, Jenesis, Grace, Michelle, Jessa, Rachel, Jacob, Griffin and the rest of my peeps at Starbucks #9413, your encouragement, and the gallons of coffee, you've given me when I sit and write in my community Starbucks have helped tremendously.

Amazing Beta Readers: Brian, Dianne, Hans, Joe, Joshua, Kim, Mark and Kelly.

Everyone who purchased and read Awakening, especially those who took the time to write reviews on Amazon—that really helps.

Joe Bonamassa, I've listened to a lot of your music during the writing of this book.

And last but not least, my editor, Joe Scholes, who has helped me become a better storyteller.

A heartfelt ***thank you*** to everyone. Your support, inspiration and participation have all contributed to my happiness and success.

Brett Humphrey

February 2020

ABOUT THE AUTHOR

Brett Humphrey is the author of the Dragonborn Series as well as various comedic sketches, plays and many other stories he hasn't written—yet.

He has worked with children and families for thirty years and has taught in the United States and countries around the world. His passion for reading started when he was a young child and he is still an avid reader of both fiction and non-fiction. His greatest desire as an author is to create books parents will want to read to their children, hopefully using different voices for the characters.

Brett lives in Arizona with his patient and supportive wife, who encouraged him to finally sit down and write one of the stories that lives in his head.

ALSO BY BRETT HUMPHREY

Dragonborn Series:

Awakening

Return

Reunite *

* *Forthcoming*

PROLOGUE

The sun was shining brightly in the midday sky as I soared through wispy clouds. The cerulean blue sky was a shade darker than the skies on Earth so I must be flying over farmlands in Theria. The snow capped mountains to the north beckoned me to fly to them and I intended to do just that until I sensed the presence of others flying beside me.

To my left was a beautiful red dragon keeping pace with me. She was slightly bigger than I and her scarlet scales sparkled like diamonds in the bright sunlight. There was an instant connection between us and I felt a sense of love and acceptance. To my right, there was a dragon much larger than I whose scales were such a deep midnight blue they appeared black. We were instantly connected as well and the same love and acceptance came from him along with a sense of great strength. Joy burst from deep within my heart which I sent back to the two dragons who were with me.

As we flew and I basked in their presence, I realized it wasn't time for me to fly to the mountains but when I eventually did, I instinctively knew I would find what I was looking for.

We are so proud of you, son, the red dragon thought to me.

Thank you, Mother, I sent back. *I miss you.*

Son, you are King now, and you will bring healing to our land, my father sent, *your mother and I love you very much.*

As the dream began to fade, my father turned his head to look me in the eye and said, *We're alive. You must find us.*

CHAPTER ONE

Tears of joy streamed down my face and I needed time to replay the dream in my mind before opening my eyes. The same dream repeated night after night for the past month, and I always had to take a few minutes to adjust before starting my day. My parents looked just like they had in my memories, but we hadn't ever flown together like we did in my dream. Before we ever had the chance, they had been killed by their friend Dimitri when I was five years old.

My parents were dead. The worst day of my life was when an advisor delivered the devastating report that they had been killed; so why did I keep dreaming that they were alive? The last time I had a recurring dream, it was of me becoming a dragon, which turned out to be true. So, what if my parents weren't dead, but alive and being held captive? What if they really were waiting for me to rescue them? What if…? These thoughts raced through my head like rabbits running from a dog. Rather than getting my hopes up, I decided it was time to start my day.

The sun was just starting to lighten the sky as I stood and stretched my huge frame. I hadn't stopped growing and now was fifty feet from nose to tail and my unfurled wings were each twenty feet long. Shelley and Bernie made it a point to measure me each week; we were all curious to see how large I would grow. If my parents' dragons were any indication of my final size, I still had a ways to go.

I moved silently from the camp because I didn't want to wake Shelley and Bernie. Taking a refreshing drink from the nearby river, I looked over at my sleeping friends, grateful we had all survived our first battle, even though Bernie had been seriously wounded. Shuddering, I recalled how she had looked in her unicorn form, covered in blood with a gigantic axe buried in her side. Thankfully, our mentor, Gustav, had taught me *Sano*, a healing spell that we used to save Bernie's life. She was so badly wounded it took the combined power of me, Shelley, Gustav and his friend Garket to bring her back from the brink of death.

My mind raced as I thought about all of the things we experienced since coming to Middle Earth. The locals called the planet Claw, but we were such *Lord of the Rings* fans Shelley renamed it Middle Earth. Smiling to myself, I thought back to the day our parents, and the rest of the shifters who were loyal to me, came through the dimensional gate.

Three Weeks Earlier

We stood in the middle of the meadow a quarter-mile from the woods, facing east. It was midmorning and we had been there for an hour. Bernie stood to my right and Shelley to my left. Gustav stationed himself behind my right shoulder as we waited.

Shelley opened his mouth, but Bernie interrupted him before he could say anything, "Shelley, if you ask, 'how much longer?' one more time, I'm going to gag you."

"What makes you think I was going to ask that?" Shelley asked, with a comical expression on his face.

"Because you've been asking the same thing every five minutes for the past hour," Bernie said through clenched teeth. "They'll get here when they get here."

The antics of my two friends made me laugh and I knew they were doing it to help ease my nerves.

"Thanks, guys," I said. "I needed that."

Shelley pumped his fist in the air. "Yes, I won the bet!" he crowed.

Confused, I asked, "What bet?"

Bernie had the grace to blush as she answered, "We've been worried about how tightly you've been wound the last couple of days. Shelley bet me that he could get you to laugh if he acted goofy, but I told him I thought you'd snap at him. He was right, so he won the bet."

"I see, and what exactly did you wager?" I asked while looking between my two friends.

Neither of them spoke, but suddenly found the ground near their feet very interesting. They had been acting strangely around each other lately and I was going to push them to tell me what they wagered.

I felt a sudden surge of power coming from the direction of the forest in front of where we were standing. Gasping, my body tingled as if flooded with electricity.

Gustav placed his hand on my shoulder and asked, "What is it, Sire?"

"I'm not sure," I stammered. "I felt a sudden burst of energy from the forest."

"Hmmm," Gustav answered, "I believe it is time to open the gate. Sheldon, it appears the moment you have been waiting for has arrived; they are here."

Expanding my senses, I followed the surge of power back into the forest and realized it was actually emanating from the dimension where Earth is located.

"All you have to do is open a gate wide enough for your family and friends to walk through," Gustav said quietly into my ear.

I imagined an opening thirty feet wide midway into the meadow, directly across from where we were standing. The air in front of me shimmered, like heat waves rising from hot asphalt, and I watched the scene in front of us change. Suddenly, I was looking at a line of people that stretched across the open gate, my parents at the front. Bernie's parents stood next to mine and Shelley's were on their opposite side. The moment everyone saw us, they cheered and started walking forward.

Over one hundred men, women and children entered through the gate but I kept my eyes fixed on my parents. The last time they saw me, I hadn't yet transformed into my dragon form or finished growing so I know I looked different to them. But I could tell that it didn't matter. They both looked at me with love and approval and they had wide smiles on their faces. Stavros and Miriam Arktos and Fritz and Frieda Einhorn were looking at Shelley and Bernie the same way. My heart filled with pride as I looked at our families.

"Sire," Gustav whispered, "the last of our people have made their way from Earth. I suggest you close the gate without delay."

"Thank you, Gustav," I said and then concentrated on erasing the gate from the meadow. I was getting better at this and the gate rapidly disappeared.

Our parents stopped ten feet away from where we were standing. Fritz Einhorn looked over my shoulder at Gustav and then nodded. He stepped closer to me, bowed and then turned to face the crowd.

"Family, friends and those loyal to the Crown, I present to you Alister Rex, High King of Shifters. Long live the King!" Fritz shouted.

The crowd shouted back, "Long live the King!" and began cheering.

While the crowd settled, Fritz Einhorn looked at me and suggested, "Sire, you should address the crowd."

"What should I say?" I asked.

He smiled and answered, "Tell them how you feel."

I thought for a moment and held up my hands for quiet. Even when a hundred people are quiet it's still noisy, so I had to yell to be heard.

"Thank you for your loyalty to my parents King Phillip and Queen Beatrice and also for your loyalty to me. Gustav has shared with me what you all sacrificed when we fled Theria and went to Earth. I promise you that we will take back our kingdom, we will free the people of Theria and Dimitri will face justice for everything he has taken from you." I spread my hands to include Shelley and Bernie.

"Sir Arktos, Sir Einhorn and I have already vanquished one bully who was terrorizing the people on this planet, and we won't stop until we have taken down Dimitri as well. I'm honored to serve as your king and will lead us home again."

The crowd cheered even louder than before and I was overwhelmed with emotion as I watched people weep with joy at my promise.

After hugging my mom and dad and telling them about the adventures we had while on Middle Earth, I walked through the camp and talked to as many people as possible. I remembered many of them from my childhood while living in the palace. It felt strange for people to treat me so differently but I am King, so I need to get used to it. Even though we would only be camped here for a month or so, people brought everything with them they wanted to take back to Theria.

Hours later, Bernie and I sat inside my tent that had been set up on a small hill in the middle of the meadow. Fritz and Freida Einhorn had been busy in the month we had been separated and had created things that they insisted I needed now that I was going to return as king. They had hired a prop company in Hollywood to make everything needed for a movie about a dragon shifter who was going to return to his homeland and set up his kingdom. They were able to stick as close to the truth as possible and the owners of the company told them they couldn't wait for the movie to come out because they loved movies with dragons in them. They put a rush on the order and everything was designed and manufactured in time for them to depart.

"Nice speech earlier," Bernie smirked at me.

"Thanks, Sir Einhorn," I said to emphasize her title, "your parents did a great job getting all this made." I waved my hand at the tent and everything in it.

"Well, they are experts in etiquette and diplomacy, and you need all the help you can get since you are only slightly more cultured than Shelley...oof," she finished as the pillow I threw at her hit her in the side.

Smiling, I asked, "And where is the loudest member of our triad?"

Bernie looked unhappy as she answered, "He said he had to talk to his mom, but would join us when it was time for our meeting."

"What's going on with you two?" I asked and looked pointedly at Bernie.

"I'm not sure what you're talking about." Bernie blushed.

We were interrupted by Gustav entering the tent, followed closely by my parents and the rest of the Inner Circle. Shelley made his way to where Bernie and I were sitting and took the seat next to her. Everyone else filled the remaining seats in the circle.

"What are our plans, Sire?" Stavros asked as he looked at me.

I was surprised by the question and didn't have an answer.

"Um..." I began.

"If I may?" Gustav asked as he looked at me. I nodded for him to continue. "I suggest that we spend the next month helping King Alister get ready for his return to Theria. There are many things he wasn't taught during the years he was trapped in his human form. I propose we begin a daily routine of history, diplomacy, etiquette, fighting and meeting with the different types of shifters who have joined us. He needs to become familiar with his duties as King as quickly as possible."

Shelley snickered and all eyes turned to him. "I'm sorry for laughing Alister, but it looks like you're going to have to go to summer school." Bernie giggled as I gave Shelley the stink eye.

"I wasn't finished," Gustav continued. "Since a King never goes into battle without his Knights, you two will go through the same training as well."

I couldn't help laughing as the grins on my friends' faces were replaced with dejected expressions.

"That sounds like a wonderful idea, Gustav," I agreed, "but tonight we need to eat together and celebrate everything we've gone through since coming here."

"Yeah, we learned how to shift into our animal forms," Bernie began.

"Learned how to fight in our human forms," Shelley continued.

"Saved a bunch of people and killed the bad guys. It was a busy month," I concluded. Even though it was said lightheartedly, all three of us felt the weight of the senseless pain and death that we had witnessed.

The next two weeks passed in a blur as I settled into my new routine. Every day, I would awake before sunrise and fly to a nearby lake for a swim and a dragon-sized breakfast. Even though I normally only needed to eat as a dragon once or twice a week, I was using a lot of energy each day and wanted to stay full. After eating, I'd fly back to camp and begin my day in my human form. Bernie and Shelley would be waiting for me, along with a cheering crowd, and they would guard me as we spent an hour visiting with my subjects before Gustav would come get us for our lessons.

Bernie and Shelley would spar with their dads, and I would spar with Mom. Dad was a good fighter, but my mom was better. At first, I was afraid of hurting her and pulled my punches. But after she knocked me to the ground around a dozen times, I finally got the message; I had to try my best. We normally had an audience and everyone would cheer for my mom. I didn't mind and really enjoyed the time we got to spend together, even though I usually had new bruises after our sessions.

We also had daily lessons in etiquette, diplomacy, history, tactics and science. I had a lot to absorb in a short amount of time but enjoyed learning all the things we were taught. My only complaint was that I was so exhausted at the end of each day, I fell into bed without getting a chance to just hang out with Bernie and Shelley. Even though we were constantly together we didn't get a chance to talk about everything we were going through.

I finally voiced my concerns to Dad towards the end of the second week. We stood outside our tent while Mom prepared dinner. Even though we stood in silence, I found it extremely comforting to stand with him, watching the sunset. Taking a deep breath, I decided to let him know how I was feeling. "Dad, I'm not sure I can do this."

He put his arm around me and waited a moment before answering me. "After we fled to Earth, I would often watch you while you were sleeping, amazed that you had been entrusted into our care and I was your dad. Your mom and I always planned on having children, but we didn't think we were ready yet. We loved your parents and were honored when they asked us to adopt you if something happened to them. We agreed but didn't really think anything could happen, after all, they were Royal Dragons. And then suddenly they were gone, your shifter and human sides were separated, your first five years of memories were wiped and we fled to Earth to escape Dimitri. You were so small and helpless, and we knew we had to do everything we could to raise you the right way." He turned towards me and put his hand on my shoulder.

"Alister, none of us are ever completely prepared for the challenges we face in life. We do the best we can with what we have and then listen to those who love us to help us grow. I'm so proud of you. You can do this because you aren't alone. Your mom and I will always be here for you. Fritz, Frieda, Miriam, Stavros, Gustav and every person in this camp are on your side and willing to follow you wherever you lead. You also have Bernie and Shelley by your side, and that bond of friendship is as tight as any I've ever seen. You can do this because we'll help you."

I swallowed the lump in my throat as I looked down at my dad and saw a fire in his eyes. Moved by his fierce love for me and his unwavering support, I grabbed him in a tight hug and whispered, "Thanks, Dad, that helps."

Soon, I let him go and continued to tell him what else was bothering me. "There's something going on with Bernie and Shelley. There seems to be a problem between the two of them and I don't know what it is."

Dad smiled and turned back towards the setting sun. "Ah, yes —that's something we should probably talk about, but this might not be the right time."

"Why not?" I said in exasperation.

He laughed. "Because I think there are a few things Shelley and Bernie need to figure out for themselves first."

"But I hate to see them upset with each other."

"Unless I miss my guess, that won't last very long."

"Dinner's ready," Mom said as she joined us. "What's going on?"

I answered her. "I'm worried about Bernie and Shelley. They've been edgy with each other the past couple of weeks and I know something's bothering them but don't know how to help."

Mom smiled as she replied, "I'm sure it'll all work out sooner rather than later, but since you've all been working so hard I have a suggestion for you. Why don't the three of you take a couple of weeks together to explore Middle Earth? You won't get many more chances to spend time alone until we get you re-established on the throne in Theria."

"That's a great idea, Mom," I exclaimed, "do you think I'm far enough along in my studies and everyone else will go for it?"

Dad laughed. "Oh, I'm sure everyone will; after all, you are the King."

"Oh yeah," I muttered. "I keep forgetting."

Mom put her arm through mine. "Well, your Majesty, it's time for you to eat. You can make plans with Bernie and Shelley after dinner. Your dad and I get you to ourselves tonight."

"Sounds good to me," I replied as we headed into the tent to have dinner.

Present Day

Middle Earth

Wilderness

I was stopped from reliving my memories by an especially deep snore from Shelley that sounded suspiciously like a bear's roar. We'd been traveling for a week so far and it had been great to spend time with my two best friends. Whatever had been bothering Bernie and Shelley appeared to be gone and they were back to their old selves. It was fun to hang out and laugh together, and for a while, I didn't really have to face my responsibilities as King.

I decided it was time for my traveling companions to awaken and it was up to me to do it. *Hey Bernie,* I thought to her, *it's time to get up and start heading back to camp.*

Awww, c'mon, Alister, Bernie replied, *it's barely light out.*

Well, I thought you might like to watch me wake Shelley, but if you really need more beauty sleep—I'll wake you again in a few minutes.

"I'm up! I'm up!" Bernie said as she stood and brushed herself off.

For some reason, Bernie and Shelley prefer to sleep in their human forms while I always prefer to sleep in my dragon form; the ground doesn't feel as hard that way. I stretched my neck over to where Shelley was sleeping and bent my head down so my face was two feet above his. I opened my mouth and used my tongue to flick his nose until he opened his eyes.

I'm hungry, I growled and opened my mouth wider showing more teeth.

"Grahhhhk..." Shelley screamed as he crab-walked backward, trying to get away from me.

I transformed back to human and joined Bernie as we laughed at Shelley's expense.

"You should've seen the expression on your face," Bernie managed to wheeze out as she continued to laugh, "you know Alister would never really eat you."

Shelley folded his arms and glared at the two of us. "It wasn't that! Do you know how bad dragon breath smells in the morning? Not cool, dude. Not cool!"

Grinning, I answered my friend. "I'm a dragon, we don't do cool."

Bernie groaned. "Okay, what's so important that you needed to wake us up at the crack of dawn?"

"It's time to return to camp so we can plan our return to Theria. I'm starting to feel a sense of urgency and want to find out if Gustav has found any more answers in Minos' library," I explained.

Shelley started stuffing his belongings in his backpack while he replied. "For a psychopathic minotaur who oppressed the citizens of

Buttle, he kept really good records of everything he thought and did. I'm glad Gustav is the one reading through his journals instead of me."

Bernie was standing still and I could tell something was wrong. She looked over to me and Shelley and said quietly, "Minos almost killed me. If you two hadn't done what you did to heal me, I wouldn't be here right now. You two are goofballs, but you're my goofballs. Thank you again for saving me."

I was embarrassed, not because I had helped save Bernie's life, but because she kept bringing it up. Clearing my throat I said, "You're welcome, Bernie, I couldn't imagine life without you."

"I didn't really do anything," Shelley said quietly. "I'm not really good with the healing spell; Alister, Garket and Gustav did all the work."

Bernie's eyes flashed in anger as she rounded on Shelley and hit his arm. "You idiot," she seethed, "quit saying that. You helped, it took every ounce of power from everyone to bring me back."

Shelley took a step towards Bernie as he continued, his voice thick with pain, "I was so afraid and helpless, Bernie, afraid that we would lose you and I felt useless because I couldn't do more." He put both of his hands on her shoulders, "you were so brave to step in front of Garket to save his life, but don't ever do that again. I don't know what I'd do without you."

Bernie smiled shyly at Shelley as she answered. "You know I can't promise that because we're both Knights, but I will promise to be as careful as possible. Does that help?"

Shelley put his hand on Bernie's cheek. "Not really, but it will have to do."

As I stood there doing a fish out of water impression, things finally clicked into place for me as I watched my two best friends stare at each other. It now made sense why they had been acting so weird around each other. Deciding to give them a few minutes alone, I began to back away.

"Um…" I started, "I'll go make breakfast and let you know when it's done."

I'm sure they heard me but they kept staring at each other so I did the only thing possible in this situation. I beat a hasty retreat.

Theria

Dimitri's Fortress

Dimitri sat on an enormous throne centered on a dais in the Great Hall of his fortress. He was in his frost giant form and when he stood would be at least twenty feet tall. Everything about him was blue. His skin was the deep blue of a frozen lake and his massive arms, shoulders and chest were filled with muscle. His hair and beard were midnight blue and his piercing eyes were such a pale blue color they were almost white. His body radiated a biting cold and no one wanted to get within ten feet of him if they could help it. He idly twirled a crown in his left hand while his chin rested on his right fist; he was deep in thought.

A gentle cough broke the silence, but it still took a few minutes before Dimitri looked up at the person who had entered the Great Hall. He was short but powerfully built and was partially shifted into his tiger form. He walked on two legs and his face was more human than tiger so he could use his mouth to speak.

"Yes, Weston, what is it?" Dimitri mumbled.

"My lord, I am sorry to disturb your meditation, but I have news and need your direction."

Dimitri roused from his pose and leaned forward to look at his servant. "Have either Phillip or Beatrice shown any sign of waking?"

"No, my lord, they still slumber."

"Have you been able to remove even one of their scales or draw a single drop of blood from either of them?"

"I'm afraid not. While they are in their dragon forms there isn't anything we can do to harm them." Dimitri moved forward a bit more, so Weston quickly continued, "not that we've stopped trying, my lord, but so far nothing we've done has worked."

Dimitri muttered to himself. "The plan was simple. I poisoned you and Beatrice in your human forms so you'd die and I would conquer the world. It was simple Phillip but you had to go and mess it up by transforming into your dragons and sleeping instead of dying. Why do you always have to mess things up for me?"

"M..my lord?" Weston stammered.

Dimitri waved his question away, and asked, "Have you finally killed the whelp, Alister?"

"I do not have an answer to that my lord. We were able to get one of your agents into the palace before you incapacitated the King and Queen, but with the dimensional gates shut, we don't know what has been happening in other dimensions."

"Have you been able to breach the defenses on the palace? Do I finally have access to the secrets contained there?" Dimitri demanded.

The servant bowed his head in defeat. "No, my lord. We still do not know what magic is protecting the palace. We have not been able to breach its defenses."

After a minute of silence, Dimitri narrowed his eyes and continued his interrogation, his voice dripping with disdain. "And the barrier separating the Kingdom of Theria from the rest of the planet, has this finally been removed?"

Weston shook his head as he continued to stare at the ground at his feet.

Dimitri stood and grabbed the spear he had leaned against the right side of his throne. "So far, this doesn't seem like news to me. All you can do is admit failure after failure. This is nothing new, I've known you were a failure for years. You assured me that you would make progress after I removed your predecessor. You've had two years to come up with solutions. I tire of hearing the word 'no.' If you don't have anything for me other than an admission of failure, then I'm afraid I will have to look for your replacement. Do I make myself clear?"

Weston paled and took a step back when Dimitri started his tirade but straightened his shoulders and took a step forward as he answered, "Yes, my lord."

Dimitri sat back down and smiled but kept his spear in his hand. "Come now, Weston, what's the news you have for me?"

"It, ah, seems like there might have been some gate activity on Claw."

Dimitri stood in anger and shouted, "When did this happen?"

The servant held out his hands in supplication. "The first, short, disturbance was recorded close to six weeks ago. The second, longer, disturbance was recorded just three week ago."

"Why wasn't I immediately informed?" Dimitri thundered.

"It appears that the scientist who discovered the disturbances, was loyal to the King and Queen and hid the information from his supervisor. I only received the full report this morning after the traitor was subjected to intensive questioning."

"I want to speak to this scientist; I want to find out what this could mean."

"That won't be possible, my lord, he died from his questioning. His interrogator was quite thorough."

"Did we find out anything else useful from him?" Dimitri bellowed.

"Before he died, he kept repeating the phrase, 'the King is returning'."

Dimitri stood silent for a few minutes while he thought through everything Weston told him. He began to bounce the spear up and down in his hand as he spoke with his servant.

"A few of my questions seem to have answers after all. It appears that the hatchling is alive on Claw and has the ability to open gates. I will lead my army to the meadow near the palace where the cowards escaped to Claw. It's the probable place they will use to return with those who left. This will be glorious. An untested boy and a ragtag group of palace servants will face my army in battle. It will be a bloodbath and, in the end, I will be victorious and have everything I need."

"Yes, my lord, you will finally have the power to crush any opposition and rule the kingdom."

"Not only that, Weston, I will use the boy's blood to open the barriers in place around the palace and kingdom and will finally have power over the gates. Once I have conquered Claw and take the magic there for myself, the other planets will fall as well."

"It will be glorious," Weston agreed.

"Weston, who is your second in command?"

"Jeffrey, my lord."

"Good, Jeffrey will need to clean up the blood before I leave with my army."

Weston looked around in confusion before asking, "What blood?"

"The blood under your body," Dimitri said as he threw his spear. Weston was thrown backward and pinned to the floor by the force of the throw. Dimitri stalked over to him and looked down at his former servant.

"I'm tired of your incompetence and no longer have need of your services. You're fired!" Dimitri said with a smirk on his face.

Weston gasped and struggled to speak, "Long live King Alister," he gurgled with his dying breath.

Dimitri reached down and yanked out the spear. Wiping the blood off on Weston's fur he ground out, "Not if I have anything to say about it." Dimitri stalked out of the room yelling for Jeffrey.

CHAPTER TWO

Middle Earth

We sat in silence as we finished our breakfast. Bernie and Shelley had been holding hands as they walked up to the fire but hadn't looked up from their plates or said anything during the meal. As happy as I was for my friends, it would take me some time to process my feelings on their new status. It had always been the three of us since we were kids. We kept each others' deepest secrets, had been through unimaginable challenges together and even trusted each other with our lives; how would this new relationship between the two of them change the friendship dynamics for the three of us?

I looked at them closely. Shelley was the same to me as he'd always been even though now he looked like a burly lumberjack who could turn into a bear. I would have to be blind not to admit that Bernie was a beautiful young woman with an amazing sense of humor, fierce loyalty and was someone I was comfortable around.

After a few minutes of pondering, it hit me that I loved Bernie like a sister and nothing more. Shelley was a lucky guy and I hoped he knew just how lucky. I didn't feel any jealousy that Shelley was the one Bernie had chosen but this was something I was going to have to talk with my parents about. For now though, we would proceed as if nothing had changed between us; at least that was my plan.

"So, how long has this been going on between you two?" I asked.

Shelley winced at the question and I realized I sounded colder than intended.

"We didn't mean to hurt you," Bernie answered in a small voice and kept her head down, "it just happened."

Shelley looked up at me and opened his mouth, but I raised my hand before he could speak. "I'm sorry, that was harsh. Please, look at me, both of you."

Bernie looked at me, but I could tell she was worried. Shelley put his arm around Bernie's shoulder and his posture stiffened, as if preparing for an argument. I took a deep breath before continuing. "First of all, I'm not hurt, just surprised. I'm happy for you both, but curious as to when your feelings changed for each other."

Shelley sighed and looked at Bernie. "For me, it was when Bernie had that huge axe buried in her side and I thought she was going to die. I was desperate to save her and realized that I cared for her as more than just a friend."

Bernie leaned closer to Shelley. "For me, it was when we were in Buttle and Shelley would play with the kids and let them climb all over him in his bear form. They weren't scared of him and treated him more like a teddy bear than a grizzly bear."

Both Bernie and Shelley were looking worried, so I smiled at them and answered the concerns they weren't voicing. "You two are my best friends, and I'd do anything to protect my friends. That means that you had both better treat each other well. Neither of you wants to get on my bad side."

My eyes turned golden and some smoke rose from my nostrils. Bernie stuck out her tongue and Shelley punched me in the arm; I laughed.

"You almost looked scary for a second," Bernie clasped her hands in front of her chest and batted her eyes, "Shelley, save me from the mean dragon."

Shelley rolled his eyes. "As if Alister would really do anything to you, but I've got to warn you, his dragon breath is terrible."

"Finish your breakfast," I snickered, "we need to get going."

We could have flown back to the main camp, but I was enjoying our time together too much. The urgency I felt upon awakening was still there but not as demanding as it had been. We needed to get to Theria as soon as we could, but the three of us could spend a couple more days returning to camp. We laughed a lot and talked about the meaningless things friends do when they are comfortable with each other. Watching Bernie and Shelley interact with each other, it became apparent that while I loved Bernie, I wasn't in love with her. We had been traveling all morning and were around an hour away from where we'd make camp for the night. Bernie and Shelley were holding hands and walking in front of me and I was smiling to myself.

Hey Alister, Shelley sent, *I'm not sure what I'm scenting but I think it smells cat-like.*

Bernie, do you smell anything? I sent.

My nose isn't as good as either of yours; unicorns aren't known for their keen sense of smell.

Remind me again what unicorns are known for, Shelley teased.

They're known for kicking their boyfriend's butt, Bernie replied.

Shelley stopped and looked at Bernie, *I'm your boyfriend?*

Oh, for crying out loud, you two, I sighed, *can you please focus for a minute? The whole reason we're communicating telepathically is so whatever is hunting us won't know we're on to it.*

Sorry, Alister. Bernie and Shelley both responded.

Now, let's keep walking to see if we can figure out what's going on, I replied.

Why don't I turn to my unicorn to see if I can draw it out to attack me? Bernie sent.

I'm not sure that's such a good idea. I don't want to see you get hurt—Shelley started.

Sheldon Petros Arktos, Bernie began, *I am a Knight of the Realm, just as you are. Like it or not, sometimes we have to put ourselves in dangerous situations to do our jobs. I'll be fine; you and Alister have my back.* With that, Bernie transformed into her unicorn and trotted down the path towards the clearing ahead.

I don't like this, Shelley sent to me.

Let's move a little quicker, I don't like it either.

As we moved closer to the clearing we heard a roar and watched as a tiger leapt towards Bernie, intending to bring her down. Bernie reared on her hind legs and struck the tiger with her front hooves, knocking it off balance. Shelley instantly transformed into his grizzly bear and went running for the tiger while releasing a huge roar. I couldn't transform because I was still on the path and there were thick branches crossing above me, but I sprinted as fast as I could towards the clearing.

By the time I cleared the trees, Shelley and the tiger were fighting fiercely, and Bernie was striking the tiger from the side with her hooves. I transformed and was looking for an opening so I could get a shot at the tiger as well. Bernie and Shelley had things under control so I watched them fight. The tiger would swipe at Bernie with its claws but Shelley would get in the way and take the blow. Even though the tiger would rake Shelley's side, it couldn't do much damage because of his size and thick fur. Once the tiger was focused on Shelley, Bernie would strike it with her hooves or her horn. In minutes the tiger was bleeding from ragged cuts made by Shelley's claws and Bernie's horn.

After a few minutes of this, the fight went out of the tiger and it lay down on the ground, rolled over and showed its belly in submission. When it did this, it became apparent that this wasn't a regular tiger but rather a shifter. Shifting into my human form so I could stop this without further bloodshed I shouted, "Enough!" Bernie and Shelley immediately stopped their attacks, although Shelley was still growling. I walked over to my friends and stopped next to the defeated tiger.

"Shift," I commanded and watched as the tiger shifted into human form. Instead of a bloody tiger, there was now a naked, bloody man, huddled on the ground.

"Well, that's awkward," Shelley remarked after he shifted back to human.

"I'll get him something to cover himself up with, while Alister heals his wounds," Bernie said as she headed back to where she had dropped her pack on the path. She ran back over and tossed a blanket over his back. I knelt next to the bloody man and placed my hand on his shoulder.

"I'm going to heal your wounds and then we're going to talk. If you try to attack any of us again, I won't have to heal you because you'll be dead. Do you understand?" I asked sternly.

The man nodded his head, so I began healing him. While I was doing that, Bernie and Shelley hugged each other and began to heal the cuts they had received in the fight. Even though they had sustained a few minor wounds, the tiger had gotten the worst of the battle.

After a few minutes I could tell the man was healed so I asked him, "What's your name and why did you attack us?"

He sat silently, with his head bowed. I wasn't sure what else to do since he had surrendered to us, but I needed answers. Before I could ask him again, Bernie interrupted me.

Alister, please let me try. I got pretty good at asking questions during the trials for the soldiers in Buttle. Apparently it's one of my gifts as a unicorn.

Please go ahead, I want to know everything related to this shifter and why he attacked us.

Will do, she sent, *Shelley, please hold him in place.*

Bernie transformed into her unicorn and her horn began to glow. Shelley came up behind him and held his arms. He looked up in surprise and tried to back away from Bernie but Shelley held him tightly against his chest. The man was much smaller than Shelley, probably only five and a half feet tall, looked to be Asian and had a look of terror on his face. Shelley touched the man's chest with her glowing horn and then transformed back to human.

"What is your name?" Bernie asked.

"My name is Wu," he replied woodenly.

"Why did you attack us?" Bernie continued.

"I had to do something to disrupt your plans to return to Theria. Since there wasn't a way to attack the dragon, I thought if I could kill the unicorn, that would keep you from going. I didn't realize how strong the unicorn was and then the bear joined the battle. I gave up because there wasn't a way for me to be victorious."

Bernie, he didn't really answer the question, did he? I asked.

She shook her head and tried it again, "Wu, why did you need to disrupt our plans to return to Theria?"

"I had to save my family."

He's answering the questions but not completely, Shelley sent.

You're right, let me give him another dose of the horn, Bernie answered.

Shelley snickered and opened his mouth to say something, but Bernie narrowed her eyes and pointed her finger at him. He closed his mouth. She transformed into her unicorn and repeated the process with her horn, making it grow brighter before she held it against Wu's chest. She transformed back to human and started her questions again.

"Wu, I want to know the reason you attacked us. Give me the whole story," Bernie said with steel in her voice.

Beads of sweat formed on Wu's forehead and he began to shake. I could tell he was fighting the command, but it was no use. After a minute, he began to speak slowly.

"I'm a tiger shifter. There are many tiger shifters who live in snowy regions of the Kingdom of Theria. My family has served in Dimitri's court for generations. I met my wife in service, and we were raising our children to follow in our footsteps. We were happy at court and served well. Everything started to change when King Phillip and Queen Beatrice had their son. Dimitri got more secretive and stopped allowing us to travel to other parts of the kingdom. Shortly after the birth of the Prince, I was called into the Great Hall to stand before Dimitri's throne.

"While I stood, waiting for Dimitri to explain why he had summoned me, guards led in my wife and children in chains. Before I could make my way over to them, the guards restrained me as well. Dimitri looked at me and said, 'Wu, you have been a loyal retainer for many years, so I have decided to reward you.' I was confused and answered him, 'I don't understand my lord, how do you mean to reward me?' He smiled evilly and answered, 'I will reward you by not having your family executed in front of you.' 'What have my wife and children done to displease you?' I asked desperately. 'Your wife told the wife of the Captain of the Guard that she is glad Phillip and Beatrice have a son. That means she is more loyal to them than she is to me. Disloyalty will be punished.' Dimitri sneered.

"I fell to my knees and begged him to spare my family. I told him he could take my life instead if he would just let them go, my wife meant no disrespect to him by expressing joy at the birth of the Prince. He stood looking at me for a long time before he answered. 'Wu, I will give you a chance to keep your family alive. You will travel to the palace and join the staff and look for a way to kill the hatchling. I will keep your family in my tender care until you succeed.'

"Dimitri left the Great Hall with his guards and I was left alone with my family, they were still in chains. I told Mei that I would do everything in my power to keep her and the children safe and would do what Dimitri asked, for however long it took and even if it meant my death. I was able to hold each of my children and kiss my wife before the guards came back into the room and dragged them away. I left that night and made my way to the palace, where I served the King and Queen.

"I didn't want to harm the Prince, but I knew that if I didn't, my family would never survive. I couldn't take the chance that Dimitri was spying on me so I looked for opportunities to complete my mission. After the death of the King and Queen and we all left the palace to migrate to Earth, I held hope that my chance would come but it didn't. Since the location of Prince Alister was kept secret, and my searches over the years didn't yield any results, I almost lost hope of ever seeing my family again. Once we came back to Claw, I began to look for ways to fulfill my mission and save my family."

"If you did manage to kill Alister, how did you think you would ever make it back to Theria?" Bernie continued.

"Before I left Dimitri's palace, I was informed that there was a shifter on Claw, named Minos who could assist me if Prince Alister ever went there. I figured he would get me back to Theria if I gave him proof of the Prince's death."

We were stunned by what Wu had told us. After a bit, Bernie asked another question.

"Wu, what do you want now?"

He bowed his head and said softly, "I want you to tell my family that I'm sorry I failed them. I never wanted any harm to come to them or to Prince Alister. If I could have stood against Dimitri, I would have, but I was afraid for my wife and children. Please kill me quickly, I deserve to suffer for my crimes, but would prefer not to."

Bernie's hand was glowing as she put it on Wu's head. She used the *Somnum* spell, and Wu promptly fell asleep.

We were silent as we stood and looked down at the sleeping man. Shelley was the first to break the silence.

"That was awesome," he enthused, "I didn't know you could do that glowy thing with your horn. You totally made him tell the truth and then put him to sleep. Wait, you've never done that to me have you?" Bernie just looked at Shelley and smiled.

"Not cool," Shelley said shaking his head, "not cool."

As usual, Shelley helped break the tension during a stressful situation, so I patted his shoulder and said, "Thanks, dude."

"What?" Shelley asked, but I could tell by the look in his eyes he knew what I meant.

Bernie leaned over and kissed Shelley on the cheek and whispered, "Thank you for being you, you big goof." Shelley blushed.

I took a deep, cleansing breath before speaking. "Well, I guess we can figure out where Minos learned to take families hostage to force compliance."

"If we didn't already know that Dimitri was a bad guy, Wu's story would have convinced us," Shelley said.

"I wonder how many other people back at the camp are working for Dimitri?" Bernie asked.

"Bernie, I'm going to need you to interview every person when we get back. That way we can make sure we don't have any more spies in camp."

Bernie nodded and looked at the sleeping man. "How terrible it must be for Wu to be separated from his family, not knowing if they're safe, or even alive. It must have been bad enough when we were all on Theria; but we've been gone for a long time." Bernie looked at me. "What if Dimitri already killed his family because we were able to safely escape to Earth all those years ago?"

I shook my head. "We won't know until we defeat Dimitri. From everything Gustav has said, there wasn't a way to communicate across dimensions when the gates were shut. We'll just have to hope they're safe and then help them when we can."

Bernie nodded and a single tear trailed down her face. I did the only thing I could and hugged my friend.

"This is horrible, Alister," Bernie whispered. "Wu's family has been imprisoned for so long."

I squeezed Bernie one last time and stepped away. "This is just one more crime Dimitri will answer for." I looked at Shelley to see if he was bothered that I had hugged Bernie, but he just had a determined look on his face as he looked me in the eyes.

"What are we going to do with him?" Shelley asked as he pointed down at Wu's immobile body.

I thought a moment before answering, "My Knights, I need advice. What do you recommend I do?"

"This stuff just got real, didn't it?" Shelley muttered to Bernie and she nodded. "We all heard him admit that he was trying to kill us. He attacked Bernie and hurt her, he should pay for that."

"He wasn't able to really hurt me," Bernie retorted, "and I'm already healed."

"But what if I wasn't close? What if I were unable to help you? What would have happened to you then?" Shelley shot back.

"But you were. Besides, didn't you see that I was holding my own? I'm perfectly capable of taking care of myself. The horn isn't for show, you know," Bernie said hotly.

"I know, you've told me a hundred times. But do you know how it makes me feel when I see you get hurt?" Shelley retorted.

"Yes, I do know," Bernie said softly as she stepped closer to Shelley. "I watched this tiger," she pointed to Wu "tear into you with his claws. You came barreling in to save me, but you weren't really thinking about what you were doing. He could have really hurt you too, Shelley."

"But he didn't, I'm fine," Shelley asserted.

"And, so am I," Bernie finished with her hands on her hips. Both of them were breathing heavily as they stared at each other.

They both looked at me in surprise as I muttered, "You've gotten a bit off topic, haven't you?"

After a few seconds, I nudged Wu with my toe and said, "You can stop pretending you're still asleep."

Wu kept his eyes closed while he muttered, "Are they always like this?"

"No, but it appears they've got some things to work out. It seems like you bring out the worst in them."

Wu nodded grimly as he stood. "Another thing I must apologize for. They woke me with their shouting, but I must say, I'm surprised that I awoke at all. Why did you not execute me for my crimes?"

I studied Wu for a moment before answering him. He was nervous but stood proudly as he held Bernie's blanket closed with one hand. His wounds were healed but he was still smeared with blood from the fight. He looked resigned as he waited for my answer.

"There are two reasons, Wu. The first is, I would never execute someone in their sleep. If you deserve to pay for your crimes with your life, you would be aware of the sentence before it was carried out. But the most important reason is—I haven't decided what I'm going to do with you yet."

Wu bobbed his head. "Then you are more honorable and merciful than I. This morning, if I had the opportunity, I would have killed you in your sleep to save my family."

"Then why didn't you?" Shelley growled and looked like he was a nanosecond away from shifting.

"Peace, bear, I meant no disrespect. In fact, I was trying to show respect to the King by admitting he has more honor than I do." Wu bowed towards Shelley and then turned towards me and bowed even lower before continuing, "I was unable to sneak into your camp because the King chooses to sleep in his dragon form."

Is that why you always transform into your dragon to sleep? Shelley sent to me and Bernie.

Not really, I answered, *but it is safer for all of us if I sleep that way since I'm more alert in my dragon form. But, the truth is, it's just more comfortable. I'm not bothered by rocky ground in my dragon scales.*

Bernie's laughter echoed through her sending. *So you're saying our lives were saved because you wanted to be comfortable?*

Yep, that sums it up. Bernie, I continued, *please keep checking whether Wu is telling the truth as I interrogate him.*

Wu stood stiffly as he watched our silent exchange. I assumed he thought we were discussing his fate. "Wu," I began, "what would happen to your family if you were executed?"

Wu hung his head in shame. "I am afraid they would be killed if they aren't dead already."

"But didn't Dimitri promise to keep them alive if you did what he ordered you to do?" Bernie asked.

"He isn't known for keeping his word," Wu answered.

"If you haven't received new orders in over thirteen years, and you aren't sure if any members of your family are still alive, why did you attack us today?" I asked.

Wu looked at me with tears streaming down his face as he answered. "King Alister, I knew there wasn't any way to defeat you so the best I could hope for is to cause you enough grief that you would kill me at once. There isn't any way for me to get back to my family so I hoped that you would kill me and I could wait for them in the afterlife."

Bernie, I sent, *is he telling the truth?*

He is, she responded.

This is so messed up, Shelley added, *what are you going to do?*

I sighed and said out loud, "What I have to do. Sirs Einhorn and

Arktos, please come stand behind me." Bernie stood behind my right shoulder and Shelley stood behind my left. Rising to my full height and putting the weight of my authority as King behind my words, I declared, "Wu, of the Northern Tigers prepare for my judgment."

Wu looked at me and stood, looking as presentable as possible while holding the blanket he still had wrapped around his body.

"You will accept my judgment for your crimes," I commanded.

"Yes, your Majesty," Wu nodded.

"Very well. For the crime of plotting to murder our royal person, your life is forfeit. For the crime of attacking Sir Bernadette Einhorn, a Knight of the Realm, in an unprovoked attack, your life is forfeit. What do you say to these charges and the punishment I have decreed?"

Wu's face was pale and he had sweat running off his forehead as he answered. "Your punishment is just, King Alister. I have dishonored myself, my wife, my children and you as the rightful ruler of the shifters on Theria. I have no right to ask, but if they still live, please let my wife and children know I never stopped loving them."

I nodded to Wu before continuing. "You will be able to tell them yourself after we defeat Dimitri and rescue your family and any others he has imprisoned."

Wu looked confused as he searched my face and the faces of my Knights standing behind me. "I don't understand, you said my life was forfeit."

I smiled and responded, "You forfeit the life you were living while you followed Dimitri's orders, but I will give you a chance to regain your life and honor by serving me. Your life belongs to me now."

Wu fell to his knees before me and bowed his head. "But why? Why would you do this for me?"

I placed my hand on his head and answered, "Wu, you know more concerning Dimitri's schemes than we do and I need you to serve as an advisor for my Inner Circle. You came to me in dishonor. I want to give you the opportunity to regain your honor and help us defeat Dimitri at the same time. His evil must be stopped, and you will help us accomplish that."

I could hear the smile in Shelley's voice as he spoke to Wu. "Dude, get up, you're one of us now. And to be completely honest, I'm concerned that you're going to lose the blanket and I do not need to see any of that again."

Wu looked startled for a few seconds and then laughed at Shelley's remark. He sobered again as he looked over my right shoulder and spoke to Bernie. "Please forgive me for attacking you. I am glad to know you aren't hurt."

"Thank you Wu, I forgive you," Bernie answered, "but I agree with Shelley, this could get embarrassing, so please stand up."

Wu looked at me and I smiled while pointing with my thumb over my shoulder, "What she said."

He smiled and took my right hand as I held it out to him and helped him stand.

Shelley stepped from behind me and clapped his hands, "Well, I don't know about the rest of you but I'm getting hungry. Let's make some lunch. Alister, if I remember correctly, it's your turn to make it."

"But I made breakfast," I complained.

Wu was shocked and he blurted out, "You would make the King prepare food for you? That's improper."

"You sound like my dad," Bernie smiled as she took a step towards Wu.

I smiled at the expression on Wu's face. "Don't worry, Wu. Bernie and Shelley have been my best friends my whole life. I let them get away with things like this because it would be too much work to train new friends to replace them."

"Don't fool yourself," Shelley called over his shoulder as he walked away, "no one else would put up with your dragon breath in the morning."

"That's true," Bernie called out to Shelley, "but I have to put up with Alister's dragon breath and your bear farts."

Wu looked back and forth between my friends and me in confusion. "Sire, I will be happy to prepare food for the three of you, it's the least I can do."

"Uh, uh, uh," Bernie said as she waggled her finger at Wu, "you, Mr. Naked, are going to find some clothes to wear before you do anything else. I'm not sure anything of Alister's or Shelley's will fit you, but we will make something work." She put her arm around Wu's shoulders and moved away with him. She kept talking to him in a stage whisper, "Besides, it's good for Alister to get his hands dirty as he serves others, it will make him a better king." Bernie looked over her shoulder and winked at me.

"Fine," I huffed, "I'll just take a quick flight to get us something to eat. I hope you like your meat well done." I transformed and launched into the sky to hunt for some lunch.

After we finished the delicious lunch I prepared, we decided to cut our trip short and fly back to camp. There was plenty of room on my back for my passengers and I flew as rapidly as possible so we could make it in time for dinner, but not so fast that anyone would be uncomfortable. Shelley sat behind Bernie and Wu sat behind Shelley. I could often hear Shelley grumble that Wu was holding on too tightly during the journey and it made me laugh every time. We talked to each other using thought-speech during the flight. I had to admit it made conversations easier that way and I didn't get bored while flying.

I rode the thermal currents as I slowly circled the main camp. The multicolored tents were arrayed in a circle surrounding my tent which was set up on a small hill. It was amazing to see how easily everyone had adapted to camping outdoors after coming to Middle Earth. These families had left homes and comfortable surroundings to live rough in a camp. Flags and banners snapped in the breeze, all of them depicting my royal crest, a crimson dragon in flight against a field of green.

We were close enough to the ground now that we could see the people below waving to us. Most were in their human forms but many of the children were in their natural shapes. I had gotten used to seeing so many different types of shifters, so I wasn't surprised to see manticores, wolves, harpies, phoenixes, centaurs, pegasuses and other creatures playing together in the meadow below. I was filled with a renewed sense of determination that I would protect my people from Dimitri and others who would wish to do them harm.

Mom, I sent, *I'm going to land near our tent in a few minutes. Can you please ask the others to gather? I need counsel.*

Of course honey, she replied, *is everything okay? We didn't expect your return for another week or so.*

We're okay, but I would rather explain to everyone at the same time. Has Gustav returned from Buttle yet?

Yes, he returned this morning.

Good, can you please make sure he is in attendance as well?

I'll see you in a few minutes.

I broke the mental connection and began to circle lower as I headed towards my tent. *This is your captain speaking, I hope you've enjoyed your flight on Alister Air. As we prepare to land, please make sure your tray tables are stowed and your seat backs are in their proper position. Hold on tight, because if you fall now, it's your own fault.* As I dove towards an open field near my tent, Bernie and Shelley whooped in delight but Wu groaned pitifully. I didn't do it to be mean, but couldn't help laughing when I heard him mutter, "Tigers aren't meant to fly."

Bernie and Shelley jumped off, and Wu fell off, when I landed and transformed. Bernie reached down and helped Wu off the ground and we walked to the tent together. I smelled the tantalizing scent of roasting meat when we entered, and Mom greeted us with hugs.

"I hope you're hungry," she said, "because I've finished roasting a bayak for dinner." She looked puzzled when she saw Wu standing between Bernie and Shelley, "It's Wu, isn't it?"

He nodded and bowed as he replied, "You are correct, m'lady, I'm surprised you remembered after all this time."

Mom smiled at him. "There's plenty of food, please make yourself at home. Everyone else will be here soon."

She stepped back and gestured for all of us to enter and we sat at the table. Mom carved pieces of meat onto platters and handed them to us.

"Thanks, Mrs. Drake," Bernie said as she took a platter, "I'm pretty hungry so I figure Alister must be famished."

"I am," I replied, "it takes a lot of energy to fly, especially with passengers."

"Wait," Shelley said with his fork halfway to his mouth, "did you just call me fat?"

"What?" I said, "I didn't say you were fat; I just said it takes a lot of energy to fly with passengers."

"It sounded to me like you called me fat, I'm not sure how that makes me feel," Shelley sounded affronted.

Bernie hid a snicker behind her hand at his antics.

"I think you should feel lucky that I'm so willing to carry your big butt on my back when I fly," I responded.

"Big butt," Shelley practically shouted with his mouth full of food. "Now I know you're making fun of me. My butt isn't big, it's perfectly proportioned for my awesomeness."

"If you're so perfectly proportioned, maybe you'd like to prove it in the ring when we finish eating," I challenged.

"You're on. I hope you're ready for a royal smackdown, your lowness," Shelley thundered as he pounded his fist on the table.

We smiled at each other and got back to eating.

"Wu, would you like more?" Mom asked as Wu sat, mouth open watching the two of us banter back and forth. He nodded absently so Mom added more meat to his plate.

Bernie placed her hand on his arm and spoke softly, "You'll get used to this after a while, they like to give each other a hard time. They're not really upset."

"Bernie's right," Mom added, "the boys like to wrestle and it makes it more fun for them if they talk a bit of smack to each other before they do. I'm sure I don't know where Alister gets his competitive nature from," Mom said with a twinkle in her eye. She turned towards Bernie as she continued, "I'm going to bet on Alister for the win, I'll assume you'll choose Shelley?"

Bernie blushed and nodded her head. "That's nice dear," Mom said, "loser of the bet does dishes. Now, who wants pie?"

CHAPTER THREE

Bernie was finishing the dishes as we gathered for our meeting. We were starting later than planned because it had taken Shelley and me longer than usual to determine a winner. We were both much stronger and had increased stamina so we gave each other quite the beat-down. Our clothes were grass-stained, ripped and a bit bloody. Shelley had accidentally split my lip with his forehead and my mouth was still healing. It was fascinating to watch the bruises on his face disappearing as we sat there. We were grinning at each other and feeling quite pleased about the match.

"Your Majesty," Fritz Einhorn began, "while I thoroughly enjoyed the spectacle of you and Sir Arktos wrestling, I am going to assume that isn't why you called this council meeting, correct?"

I nodded, stood, stretched and groaned as the vertebrae in my back popped back into place. "Thank you all for coming on such short notice, there are quite a few things we need to tell you and then we need to figure out what we're going to do next."

I started with the dream I'd been having about my parents being alive. Bernie and Shelley told the tale of Wu's attack, and Shelley didn't embellish too much. When Bernie finished the dishes she sat between her parents and as Bernie added her version of the story, the looks they gave Wu weren't friendly.

Wu told his tale next and I watched the faces of everyone in the room as he spoke. They still displayed anger but now instead of being angry with Wu, they turned their anger towards Dimitri, where it belonged. When Wu finished, Bernie let everyone know the judgment I had levied against Wu and they nodded in agreement. We took a break after that to stretch our legs and grab something to drink.

Shelley came up to me and said quietly, "I'm really grateful for our quick healing ability, I was feeling really sore after our match."

"Me, too," I agreed, "I'm pretty sure you cracked my rib."

Shelley chuckled, "Just because you're the king, it doesn't mean I'm going to make things easier for you."

"I'm glad," I responded, "it's important for you and Bernie to treat me the way you always have. It would be easy for me to lose myself with the way everyone looks to me for answers."

"Don't worry dude," Shelley grinned, "we're more than happy to keep you grounded."

"Thanks, Shelley. I mean it," I said gratefully and looked over to where Bernie was standing between her parents. "Is it just me, or are Bernie's parents keeping the two of you separated tonight?"

Shelley sighed. "It's not just you. I guess this is something we'll have to discuss. Probably not tonight though, we've got more important things to cover right now."

Nodding in agreement I added, "But you and Bernie are also important to me. We'll talk about this, at the right time."

We took our seats and Gustav turned towards me. "Sire, I have news and would like to share next." I nodded to Gustav and he addressed everyone in the room.

"As you know, my friend Garket and I have been spending time in Buttle searching through Minos' library to see if we could discover anything concerning his plans. What we found aligns with everything Wu has shared with us. Unlike Wu, Minos was a willing participant in Dimitri's plan and had been part of his deceit for years. Not only did we find his correspondence with Dimitri before the gates were closed, but I also found detailed plans of how Dimitri planned to conquer Middle Earth."

"I am sorry to interrupt," Wu began, "but what is Middle Earth?"

Stavros held up his hand before Shelley could speak, "King Alister and his Knights, renamed Claw, Middle Earth."

Wu nodded to himself, "Then I will call it Middle Earth as well."

I leaned towards Shelley. "Dude, why didn't you learn how to tell a story from your dad? He can give a lot of information with just a few words."

Shelley looked over at his dad who was smiling smugly. "Yeah, but it's a lot more exciting when I tell it."

Gustav interrupted us before we could get going. "Even though the plans are over thirteen years old, I believe they should concern us because we could be facing Dimitri's entire army if we open the gate in this meadow to return to Theria."

"But, Gustav," I began, "we need to get back to Theria immediately. Not only do we have to defeat Dimitri, but I also have to know if my dreams are true and my parents are alive."

Mom and Dad came to stand on either side of me and each put a hand on my shoulder. "Son," Dad began, "it would give me the greatest pleasure if your parents were still alive, but we need to use wisdom as we make our plans."

Mom continued, "You would survive an encounter with Dimitri and his army but since we don't know how many shifters we would be facing we need more information before we attack."

I sighed, "You're right, but I hate the thought that Dimitri will be allowed to harm our people one second more than necessary. Gustav, what do you recommend?"

"I recommend we travel to the corresponding landmass on this planet and open a gate to Eutheria."

There were groans from many of the people in the room when Gustav suggested this.

"I know that the current ruler in Eutheria can be a bit difficult to deal with, but I believe we will need to gather allies before we return to Theria to confront Dimitri."

Shelley raised his hand, which made Gustav smile before he asked his question. "Um, Gustav, I'm a bit confused...actually, I'm really confused. It seems like I should know the name Eutheria but I can't remember where I've heard it before."

Miriam Arktos spoke before Gustav could. "Perhaps I can help. Our planet is called Theria and it is divided into seven kingdoms, each of those kingdoms is ruled by its own royal family. The Kingdom of Theria is the High Kingdom and is where the High King rules. You haven't properly covered the geography of Theria in your lessons yet, so I will link each kingdom to its corresponding continents on Earth.

"The Kingdom of Theria covers North America, Metatheria covers South America, Eutheria covers Europe."

"Although the current ruling idiot renamed it Draconia," Mom interrupted with venom in her voice.

Everyone except Bernie, Shelley, Wu and I laughed at that so we looked at each other and shrugged our shoulders.

Miriam continued, "As I was saying, Carnivora covers Africa, Sirenea covers Asia, Marsupia covers Australia, and Cetacea covers what would have been the area of Atlantis if it hadn't sunk into the sea."

"You mean, there really was an Atlantis on Earth?" Bernie asked.

Fiona patted her hand. "Of course, dear. It was actually one of our most important research facilities before an unfortunate accident."

"Wait a minute, these names sound familiar to me," I said.

"Duh, dude," Shelley said, "they're kingdoms from our home planet."

"I know, but this is the first time we're focusing on them in this way. I know I've heard some of these names before," I said.

"You're right, Alister," Bernie agreed, "I've heard them before, too."

I could see when Bernie remembered, because her face lit up with joy. "We learned these names in science class. If I'm correct, each of these names is a different class of mammals."

"You are correct, Sir Einhorn," Gustav agreed, "shifters have influenced Earth more than anyone is really aware of. Not only have our shifters given rise to the mystical creatures on Earth, but we contributed a good deal to the arts and sciences as well. As pleased as I am that you figured that out, we should get back to the topic of what we need to do next."

"Why do you think it would be safer to gate into Eutheria rather than here?" I asked.

"Two reasons," Gustav continued, "the first is, even though the current ruler of Eutheria is an idiot, as Fiona so sweetly put it, he isn't likely to have developed an alliance with Dimitri so we will be safe to travel from there. The second reason is with the right persuasion, I believe we can convince him to assist us by sending many others to fight with us when we face Dimitri and his army."

"Why would he do that?" I asked.

"Because," Mom started, "he would love to do anything to gain the gratitude of the High King. He may be a simpering, sniveling, manipulative, lying toad, but he does have ambitions. Besides, if he doesn't, I'll kick him off the throne and take over his rule."

I looked at my mom in shock; I had never seen her so angry. Dad put his arm around her shoulders and leaned towards me to explain. "It's a family matter son. Moss is the current ruler and he's your mom's younger brother. She's the rightful ruler and they hadn't spoken to each other for years, even before we left Theria." Seeing the questioning look on my face he added, "it's complicated, we'll discuss the details later."

"It just burns me to think we have to approach that...that coward for help," Mom seethed. She was lost in thought for a moment and then let out a long sigh, "but you're probably right. I don't have to like it, but I'll do it."

"Okay," I continued, "the suggestion to open a gate to Eutheria is on the table. Does anyone else have any concerns regarding this course of action?" Everyone except Shelley shook their heads. "What's your concern, Shelley?" I asked.

"If Eutheria is somewhere we would call Europe, how are we going to get there? That's like thousands of miles away from here," Shelley responded.

"Couldn't we just open a gate back to Earth, take an airplane to

Europe and open gates back to Middle Earth then open one to Eutheria?" Bernie asked.

Fritz Einhorn shook his head. "Since we're not sure if Dimitri can exploit a weakness that may be created between dimensions when the King opens a gate, we want to wait a month before we open each gate. We may be overly cautious in doing it this way, but Dimitri cannot be allowed to infect another dimension with his evil. If we traveled to Earth first it could take us three months to reach Eutheria. And then we'd have to add in the time it would take to convince Moss to help us and then travel to the Kingdom of Theria to confront Dimitri. If I understand King Alister correctly, he wants to take care of Dimitri as soon as possible."

We sat in silence while we digested what Fritz said.

Gustav continued, "I believe the wisest course of action would be to travel as quickly as we can on this planet to the landmass we would call Scotland. We can gate from there into the Kingdom of Eutheria where we connect with Moss and secure his help."

"As much as I hate to admit it," Mom huffed, "that makes the most sense."

"Well, that's settled," I said, "when can we leave and who should we take with us?"

Stavros spoke up, "I believe we should only take those of us in this room, and we can leave by the end of the week."

Everyone nodded in agreement, so he continued. "Gustav, you should return to Buttle and plan our route with Garket. See if he can give us any information in connection with any towns along our path as well as animals we'll need to hunt along the way. Fritz, Frieda and Sir Einhorn, you should speak to every person in camp to see if there are any more of Dimitri's spies among us. Since we cannot take anyone else with us, we wouldn't want to leave someone behind who is planning on causing trouble."

"What's Wu going to do?" Bernie asked.

Stavros looked at Wu as he answered. "He will come with us. While I do believe he truly wants to defeat Dimitri, his family can still be used against him. If someone was threatening my family I would do almost anything to save them. Until he proves himself, we will need to keep an eye on him."

Wu bowed his head and responded, "You are wise Great Bear, you have my word that I will not betray you. I will regain my honor by proving my loyalty to King Alister."

Stavros nodded and continued, "We will need Albert, Fiona, Gustav and King Alister to fly and the rest of us will ride in our human forms. Since they will also need to carry all our supplies, Miriam, please have harnesses and saddles created to fit our friends. It will be a long journey and we will need support while we travel. King Alister and I will work on our battle plans and organize the troops here for defense. Even though we won't open the gate from here into Theria, we still want a group of fighters on this side in case they can join the battle and attack Dimitri unaware."

"But what will I do, Dad?" Shelley asked.

"Son, unless he sends you on a mission of your own, you are to stand by the King at all times. You will be working with us as well," Stavros smiled at his son.

Shelley held out his fist for a bump. "That's what I'm talking about, Alister, I was afraid you would try to do this without my expertise."

"What expertise?" I asked, "we've never been in a battle before."

"That's true," Shelley countered, "but the hours I've spent playing video games and watching epic movie battles have to count for something."

"I'm sure they will dear," Miriam muttered, "I'm sure they will."

We discussed plans for another hour or so and then everyone left. It was decided that Wu would bunk with Gustav until he gathered his own belongings the next day, so they headed off together. When it was just Mom, Dad and me in our tent I decided to ask what had bothered her so badly during our conversation.

"Mom, why did you get so upset earlier when we were talking about your brother in Eutheria?"

Mom sighed and held Dad's hand. "Because my brother is a bigoted jerk who has no business ruling and I hate the fact we have to go to him for help of any kind."

Dad leaned over and kissed my mom on the temple and chuckled. "Love, why don't you tell Alister how you really feel?"

Mom laughed and continued, "I feel like I made the right decision in choosing you over ruling Eutheria, that's for sure."

"Let's pretend I don't know anything regarding this," I said, "and let's start from the beginning."

Mom nodded. "I was born in Eutheria and was supposed to take over ruling the kingdom when my parents abdicated. I had trained my whole life for this and had planned to follow that course when something radical changed my life. I met your father."

"Do you mean this dad?" I pointed to my dad, "Or do you mean my father, King Phillip?"

"Both," Mom laughed. "Your father, who was the Crown Prince at the time, was nearly ready to take over the rule of Theria from his father and was traveling to the other kingdoms on a goodwill mission. It was a pretty big deal and the Crown Prince would spend six months in each kingdom getting to know the rulers and people there. He also brought members of his Inner Circle with him. I met this guy," she pointed at my dad, "at the same time and we fell in love."

"I was pretty amazed that this beautiful woman would even look twice at me, let alone tell me she felt the same way about me as I felt about her," Dad admitted.

"We approached Prince Phillip for his blessing and he agreed to officiate our wedding. We were overjoyed, but my brother was not. He wanted to rule and looked for any excuse to see me removed. He found an obscure text in the archives stating that only a natural drake or natural mated pair could ascend the throne."

"But that shouldn't have been a problem because you and Dad were getting married."

"That wouldn't have been a problem, Alister, except I wasn't born a fire drake, I was born a centaur." Dad continued.

I was confused as I answered, "But you're a fire drake now, I've seen you transform."

"That's true," Mom agreed. "When a shifter finds a mate who is a different species, they can decide to perform a final shift so they can be the same species as their mate. The process is incredibly painful and cannot be reversed once performed so you have to make sure it's something you really want."

"I loved your mom and decided I would shift into a fire drake to be with her." Dad smiled as he looked at Mom.

"Yes you did, and you are a handsome man and drake," Mom purred as she looked at Dad.

I held up my hand, "Woah, you two. Can you please finish the story before I have to leave the room?" I smiled.

Mom shrugged and continued. "There's not much else to tell. Your dad underwent the transformation ceremony and we were married, blessed by Prince Phillip himself who performed the ceremony. During the reception, my brother approached our parents and told them that I was unfit to rule since I had violated the law and hadn't married a true fire drake. He further insulted us by loudly proclaiming that my new husband would always be weaker than a truly born drake. Instead of abolishing an archaic law, my parents listened to my brother as he argued his case. They knew what he was doing was wrong, but since they didn't know how to tell him no, they let the law stand."

"Why didn't Prince Phillip intervene?" I asked.

"He didn't want to override a sovereign law in another kingdom. While he agreed it was a stupid law, since it only affected the ruling family, he felt it would be better for us to change it ourselves. When I realized that this could actually cause problems for the Kingdom of Eutheria I decided to renounce my claim to the throne. Moss must have been planning for this and he pushed my father to announce his abdication and proclaim my brother to be ruler instead, and he did. This put Prince Phillip in a difficult position but since he represented the High King, he had to crown Moss on our wedding day.

“The moment my brother was crowned, he banished me and your dad and told us we could never return. I'm still a bit bitter because our wedding day was marred by my brother's grasp for power, an insult to my husband, cowardice from my parents who stood by and watched all this happen and my brother banishing me from Eutheria all for the sake of power for Moss."

"But the wedding cake was delicious," Dad smirked.

"That's true," Mom said as she laughed. "I joined Prince Phillip on the rest of his journey and haven't been back to Eutheria since."

"I'm sorry that happened to you," I said.

"Don't worry, son," Dad said, "we're happy together and this time when we stand before Moss, our adopted son is High King of Theria and he won't know how to react. He's going to kiss your mom's feet just to get in good with you."

"I'll make sure to wear nice nail polish," Mom laughed evilly.

We were finishing some late-night pie when I decided to talk to my parents regarding Shelley and Bernie. "Um, I was hoping to talk with you—uh, well, you see..."

Mom put me out of my misery and broached the subject. "So, Alister, it looks like Bernie and Shelley are really getting along."

Dad snorted at Moms lack of subtlety and she gave him a look. "Albert, dear, our son was having a bit of trouble getting the words out so I decided to help him. That's not a problem, is it?"

Dad shook his head. "Not at all, I just love watching you work. I've missed your 'bludgeon things until they quit bothering you' approach to life; it's good to see you back on your game."

"Thank you, I think," Mom replied, "now, where were we?"

"You were gently bringing up Bernie and Shelley's feelings for each other," Dad smirked.

Mom laughed and smacked Dad on the arm, "I'll deal with you later."

"Is that a promise?" Dad asked while waggling his eyebrows.

"Come on, I'm sitting right here," I laughed.

Mom turned serious as she stated her concern. "Alister, it's evident that Bernie and Shelley have decided to explore their feelings for each other and I imagine you're feeling conflicted about that."

I thought before answering. "I really wasn't until you told me how one shifter can transform into another type of shifter when they find their true mate."

Dad cleared his throat. "Well, that's true for all types of shifters except one, Royal Dragons."

"That figures," I grumped.

Mom stood next to me and put her arm around my shoulders. "Alister, believe it or not, this is really for the best. Let me explain," Mom said and raised a hand to stop my interruption, "you know that when you're in your dragon form, nothing can harm you except another Royal Dragon or weapons made from the scales or bones of another of your kind, correct?"

I nodded and Mom continued. "When your dad made the decision to shift from a centaur to a fire drake so we could marry, he also made a decision to always be weaker than a natural-born fire drake. This doesn't really matter to most shifters because the differences are relatively minor. But that isn't true for Royal Dragons. If, for example, Bernie were able to transform into a Royal Dragon, she would be weaker than a normal female Royal Dragon and would be a target for anyone trying to create a weapon that could kill you in your dragon form. She would always have to be on guard against enemies and would be vulnerable. Not only that, but you would also remain constantly vigilant and that could eventually steal your happiness. The two of you could begin to resent one another because you had to live your lives that way."

"That would be a terrible way to live," I said and thought through the implications.

"Fortunately, that cannot happen, and Royal Dragons can only be born the natural way."

"Do I need to give you the 'talk' son, regarding what your mom is telling you?" Dad asked as he once again waggled his eyebrows.

I laughed. "No, that's okay, we already covered that last year, thank you very much."

"I'm here if you need me," Dad chuckled.

"So, if you and Dad have kids, will they also be weaker than regular fire drakes?" I asked.

"No," Dad replied, "the weaknesses aren't passed along to the children."

"This is important information," Mom said, "but I really want to know how you're feeling in regard to Bernie and Shelley."

"Believe it or not, I'm really happy for them, I was surprised at first, but it makes perfect sense. We've been close for years, so it's only natural for them to develop feelings for each other. I asked them when they knew they liked each other as more than friends, and they had good answers. For Shelley, it was when Bernie almost died and for Bernie, it was when Shelley was playing with the kids in Buttle."

"Are you concerned how this could affect your friendship?" Dad asked.

"A little," I answered, "but, the more I thought through their feelings for each other the more I realized my love for Bernie is like a sister; I'm not in love with Bernie, and I'm not in love with Shelley either," I joked. "I'm not sure if they're true mates or not, but as long as we all remain friends, it won't be a problem for me."

"That's a very mature attitude, Alister," Mom complimented me.

"Thank you. I'm learning that as King, I have to make mature decisions, whether I want to or not."

"That's true," Dad added, "but don't forget to have fun along the way."

"Oh, I will," I replied, "for now, I'll imagine what Shelley would look like as a unicorn."

"Why would you do that?" Mom asked.

"Because, if Bernie and Shelley are true mates, I can't see Bernie ever giving up being a unicorn, can you?" I laughed.

Mom and Dad must have pictured what Shelley would look like as a unicorn as well because they both cracked up.

The next morning we began preparing for our journey. Each member of the Inner Circle took care of their assigned tasks while Shelley and I met with his dad to receive a crash course on battle strategy. It was actually fascinating to learn the strengths of the different types of shifters and how to best utilize those strengths in battle. Cat shifters were the fastest and would be used to circle the enemy and try to come at them from the sides and behind. They were also used to take out the enemy cats. Centaurs were used as archers and also for melee combat as the enemy troops got closer. Giants, while very strong, were typically slow so they were used as artillery and would throw boulders at the enemy army. Bear shifters could soak up a lot of damage so they were used as tanks and would typically be on the front line and charge into the enemy. Pack shifters, like wolves, were used to take down enemy bears. Those shifters with power like manticore, basilisks, chimera, banshee, gorgons, minotaur, lamia and others, would use their special skills against the enemy.

If the armies were closely matched, the deciding factor would usually be air support. Flying shifters would drop heavy objects over the enemy line to incapacitate the leaders and other key targets. If the flying shifters were fire or ice breathers, they would use those skills as well. Shifter battles were long, bloody and frequently left both armies decimated. The largest army with the best tactics was usually the victor but the loss of life was staggering. According to Stavros, there hadn't been a true shifter war for over three thousand years since the unification of Theria under the first High King and Queen.

"Dad," Shelley said, "this is great information and all, but we have Alister."

"King Alister," Stavros interrupted.

"King Alister," Shelley nodded in agreement, "why don't we just have him fight the other army. They don't have anything that can hurt him, right?"

"You are correct, but what would happen if the King fought the army by himself?"

"He would decimate them, no one could stop him," Shelley answered.

Stavros nodded as he looked at me. "The only reason the kingdoms were united is that King Alister's ancestors cared more for their people than they did about their own power. A male Royal Dragon from Eutheria and a female Royal Dragon from Sirenea joined together in a marriage alliance, conquered the other kingdoms and set up the unified kingdom in Theria. They didn't have to fight battles once they were united because everyone knew there was no way to stop them. Instead of the path of war, they chose the path of peace and benevolence. They chose to serve their people rather than use their power to keep them down. There are two reasons that it would be unwise for King Alister to wipe out Dimitri and his army. The first is it would violate everything his family stands for."

"*Protect the Weak*," I said.

"Yes, Sire, *Protect the Weak*," Stavros agreed, "we don't know what holds Dimitri has over the soldiers in his army but it's more than likely their families are being held hostage. This seems to be a pattern of his. You could destroy the army, but would you be able to live with yourself if you did?"

I shook my head. "And what is the second reason?"

"It is possible that Dimitri found a way to turn your parents' bodies into weapons," he held up his hand to forestall my response, "I know you believe they may still be alive, but it is my job to think through all possibilities to keep you safe."

"I understand, and don't want to get my hopes up too much, but we cannot completely ignore the message from my dream."

"I wouldn't ask you to, Sire," Stavros replied quietly.

"But what about Dimitri?" Shelley asked. "Can King Alister destroy him?"

"Oh, yes," Stavros replied with an evil gleam in his eye. "It would be quite appropriate for the King to destroy him."

"There will be no escape for Dimitri," I growled, "he has used his power to betray those he promised to serve. He took my parents from me for all these years and he has harmed the people who were entrusted in his care. Dimitri sealed his doom when he imprisoned

Wu's family and his crimes have continued to pile up since that time. Dimitri's reign of terror must be brought to an end."

I turned towards Stavros and said in my most solemn tone, "Stavros Arktos, I charge you with the recruitment, training and protection of my army. You will create and implement the strategies necessary for us to win the battle with the fewest number of casualties to either side. Do you accept this charge?"

Stavros turned to me, drew his sword and knelt down. He held his sword in his right hand and transformed his left hand into a bear's paw.

"Your Majesty," he growled, "I accept this charge and offer you my sword, my claws and the battle wisdom gained over my long years of service. Upon my life, I swear to keep your people as safe as possible, both those who are with us and those who are against us."

"Rise, General Arktos, I trust you to lead our people to victory, but you will leave Dimitri to me."

"It will be as you say, Sire," Stavros replied, "and it will be my pleasure."

CHAPTER FOUR

The next day we met again in my tent to discuss our plans. Gustav had returned from Buttle late the night before and came in as we were sitting down.

"I worked with Garket to map out our journey," Gustav explained during breakfast as he rolled out two maps. The first map was from Earth and the second was a partial map from Middle Earth. Gustav started by tracing the route on the map from Earth.

"As you know, we left Earth in the wilderness of Maine and we need to get to the area that corresponds to Edinburgh, Scotland before we create a gate into Theria."

"Woah," Shelley moaned, "how many miles is that?"

Gustav paused a moment in thought before he answered Shelley. "If we could fly in a straight line, it would be roughly twenty-nine-hundred miles. Unfortunately, we won't be able to fly in a straight line because we would travel most of the way over the ocean. I'm not sure even King Alister could cover the distance in one flight. And I know neither Albert, Fiona nor I can."

We decided that I would carry Shelley, Bernie and most of our gear. Mom would carry Stavros and Miriam, Dad would carry Fritz and Frieda and Gustav would carry Wu.

"What other options do we have?" I asked.

"I propose that we follow this path instead," Gustav continued to trace the new path as he spoke. "To make it easier, I will just use the Earth names for the places we'll travel, agreed?"

We all nodded.

"We will fly north into Canada and head towards the Northwestern Passages. When we reach the coast we will make our way northeast over the Labrador Sea towards Nunavut, Canada. From there, we will fly over to Greenland and then to Iceland. From Iceland, we will head over to the Faroe Islands and from there to Scotland. We can break up the journey this way and the longest leg will be approximately five hundred and sixty miles."

"That's not so bad," Shelley said brightly, "twenty-nine hundred divided by six hundred is only five flights."

"Actually it will be much farther than that," Gustav commented. "If the straight line is twenty-nine hundred miles the route we will have to take will be much longer. By my estimation, it will be a little over four thousand miles."

Everyone was silent while we digested this information. I leaned over the map and traced the proposed journey. I could see where Gustav had already made marks which I assumed would be stopping points.

"It looks like the longest leg will still be over water, is that correct?" I asked.

"Yes," Gustav answered, "there isn't really another way around that portion of the journey. We will have to build up our stamina so we will be able to fly over six hundred miles without stopping."

"Okay," I nodded, "then that's what we'll have to do. How do you suggest we proceed?"

Gustav pulled out the partially completed map of Middle Earth and traced a line he had drawn. "From our camp to Buttle it is roughly one hundred miles. I can fly there in ninety minutes, but I'm not really flying very fast. Yesterday, Garket and I flew along the route we will take and placed markers, one hundred, two hundred and three hundred miles out from Buttle.

“After breakfast, I suggest those of us who can fly should attempt to make it to the furthest marker and then fly back to Buttle. That way we can determine how far we can travel without stopping. If we can make it to the furthest marker and back to Buttle we will have traveled seven hundred miles. We'll rest in Buttle and then fly back here. Tomorrow we will repeat the exercise but with passengers and supplies. We will keep doing this every day until we feel comfortable enough to make the whole journey."

"What will the rest of us do today while you're gone?" Shelley asked.

"We will continue our preparations," Miriam said, "we still need to complete the saddles, figure out a way to carry our supplies and find ways to keep warm on the journey."

"We won't need to fly very high for most of the trip but we will need to cross a few mountains and it will definitely be cold over the ocean," Gustav commented.

"At least we're not trying to make this journey in winter," Frieda added. "That would really be bad."

"We can keep our riders warm by keeping our fire stoked," Mom replied.

“Unfortunately that won't work for Wu since Gustav doesn't have fire,” Frieda added.

“As a tiger, I am used to the cold. I can partially shift to help keep myself warm,” Wu explained.

“That's helpful,” Miriam said, “but perhaps coats would be good as well."

"Wu, Miriam, Shelley and I will hunt some of the bayak for meat." Stavros stated.

"We will ask people in camp for materials we can utilize to create what we’ll need then organize a team to work on the saddles so we can have them finished by tomorrow. We'll also need to create some sort of harness system so King Alister can carry all our supplies," Frieda said.

Shelley turned to me with a grin on his face and slapped me on the back. "Well, Stretch, it seems like you get to have all the fun flying for hundreds of miles while I have to stay back here and hunt bayak. If possible, I would take your place. But, since bears can't fly, I guess it's up to you."

Bernie spoke up before I could, "Hey, Shelley? You know how bored you were on the three-hour car ride up here?"

Shelley nodded and grimaced at the memory.

"While you're hunting today, just think how bored you're going to get on a four-thousand-mile journey," Bernie smiled sweetly.

Everyone laughed at the expression on Shelley's face.

"Yup," I snickered, "get your exercise today because you won't have many chances until we get to where we're going."

"Me and my big mouth," Shelley muttered.

We spent the rest of the week preparing for the journey and I have never been more exhausted in my life. Gustav taught us the *Dies* spell which allowed us to keep track of the amount of time we spent while flying. By doing this, we were able to get a good idea of our speed. Everyone was comfortable keeping a pace of a hundred miles an hour. We would have to see how that speed felt to our passengers.

The first day we were able to travel around three hundred miles before Gustav had to stop to rest. We rested for four hours and then made the return journey. By the time we made it back to camp, we could barely walk after we shifted to our human forms. We were grateful someone else had cooked for us but Dad fell asleep before he finished eating.

The next day we loaded our passengers and tried again. Thankfully, my shifter healing had kicked in so I wasn't sore when we started the day. However, by the time we finished, it was once again difficult to walk. We were able to cover four hundred miles in a four-hour round trip but Mom, Dad and Gustav collapsed when we landed back at camp. They had to recuperate in the landing zone for nearly an hour before they could shift. I brought back a bayak for each of them and it was funny to watch them trying to eat the animal while lying down.

Our passengers were cramped, grumpy and windblown when we returned but all in all, we'd done better than the day before.

We were finally able to successfully complete six hundred miles in six hours without stopping the fourth day of practice. Our passengers found goggles somewhere in camp and each of them had a pair. It was easier on the passengers when their eyes were protected. Even though there were disagreements and some conflict because each of us were so sore and tired, we felt like we accomplished something together during the week.

Once we started our journey the plan was to fly at least four hundred miles in the morning, rest for four hours and fly another four hundred miles in the afternoon. If we could keep that pace, it would take us four and a half days to reach our destination. While I wanted to gate into Theria as quickly as possible, my first concern was the safety of my people.

We decided to spend a full day resting before beginning our journey and everyone was glad for the break. I wanted to spend some time among the people who were in the main camp and asked Bernie and Shelley to come with me. The three of us walked together and Bernie and Shelley held hands.

"I'm glad we didn't find any other shifters under Dimitri's thumb when you and your parents questioned everyone," I said to Bernie as we walked.

"Me, too," she answered. "I'm not sure what we would have done if there'd been anyone else."

"Maybe they would have been like Wu," Shelley said, "and were looking for a way out."

"Do you think he has anyone who follows him willingly?" Bernie asked.

"Unfortunately, I do," I answered. "Think about Minos, he followed Dimitri because he wanted to feel superior and hold people down. He was powerful because he was a shifter among humans. The soldiers who followed him used fear, threats and violence to keep people oppressed. Dimitri draws people like that to himself because they want to tear down others and use their power to benefit themselves. It may sound simple, but they are bullies, powerful, but bullies all the same."

"And what do we do with bullies?" Shelley sing-songed.

"We stop them," the three of us said together.

"And why do we stop them?" Shelley continued.

"Because we *Protect the Weak*," we repeated in unison and laughed.

"Alister, do you really think your parents are alive?" Bernie asked and looked at me with compassion in her eyes.

"I'm not sure but hope so. I have the same dream about them every night; that has to mean something."

"But how could they still be alive after all this time?" Shelley asked.

"I don't know," I replied truthfully.

Shelley nodded and said, "Then we'll have to ask them when we find them."

Bernie hugged Shelley's arm on one side, and I hugged him on the other. "And that's why you're my best friends," I said with emotion, "you've got my back, no matter what."

"Yeah, we do," Shelley muttered, "I just wish your back wasn't so bony, it would make it a lot easier to be your friend while we're flying if you were a bit softer."

"Poor baby," Bernie teased, "maybe we should get you some pillows for the trip."

"What a great idea," Shelley exclaimed. "Maybe we'll find some in the camp that we can borrow."

We didn't get any pillows, but we did get a lot of people giving us encouragement and well wishes for our journey. Every adult in the camp had worked in the palace and many of them asked us to stop and share a meal with them. Many told me stories of my parents and how the King and Queen would often go out of their way to show kindness to them. As we talked, it was like extra memories were unlocked and I would recall different interactions with that person when I was a child. Each encounter would end with an embrace, me thanking them for their story and usually some tears.

Every story would give me a deeper sense of resolve to save these people and the rest of the shifters who were under Dimitri's evil influence.

We were content and absolutely stuffed as we started our way back up the hill to my tent. I sensed Shelley and Bernie stiffen next to me when they noticed a small figure blocking the path in front of us.

I don't think there's anything to worry about, I sent, *let's see what she wants.*

We stopped a few feet away from the girl on the path. She looked to be around eight years old, had riotous, black curly hair, dark chocolate skin and a scowl on her face. She was wearing shin guards, knee pads, and had on a long coat cinched tight around her waist with a leather belt. It also looked like she was wearing some type of hard plastic shell fastened with bungee cords at the top and the bottom, under her coat. She had painted a red dragon in flight on the shell which peeked through the opening of the coat. She also had a sheathed knife on her belt to complete her set of homemade armor.

I wasn't worried but transformed the skin on my chest and back to scales, just in case. Taking a knee so we were mostly at eye level I addressed the girl. "And what can we do for you, young warrior?"

She stared into my eyes as she said, "I want to go with you, to *Protect the Weak.*"

"What's your name?" I asked.

"I am called Mkali," she answered, "that means fierce, and I can fight," she said as she touched the hilt of the knife at her belt.

"You are certainly fierce, young one," Bernie said softly, "but it is not wise to touch a weapon in front of the King's Knights, especially when you are also in the presence of the King."

"Please forgive me, your Majesty," Mkali gasped and fell to her knees, "I meant no harm."

I looked over my shoulder and smiled at my two friends, who were smiling back at me. *"I like her,"* Shelley mouthed at me and I nodded in agreement.

"Please stand up, Mkali, there is nothing to forgive. I know you mean no harm. However, the lesson Sir Einhorn taught you is a good one to remember." I grasped her hand and continued, "Would you like to join us for refreshments as you tell us your story?"

Mkali nodded so quickly I thought her head would snap off her neck. "Very well, we must ask your parents. Which tent is theirs?" Mkali pointed to a blue tent two hundred feet away. "Sir Arktos, would you please ask Mkali's parents if she could join us? I am sure Sir Einhorn and Mkali will keep me protected while you do this."

I couldn't help smiling as Mkali stood back up and tried to mirror Bernie's stance. She looked fierce as she swiveled her head left and right looking for potential enemies. Bernie's gentle cough stopped Mkali's hand as she was about to rest it on the hilt of her knife. Mkali kept glancing at Bernie to make sure she was doing the same thing as the tall Knight. *You've got an admirer,* I sent, *it's cute.*

Cute or not, Sire, Bernie's sarcasm came through loud and clear over our mental link, *she is taking this seriously.*

Don't get me wrong, I'm not mocking her; I am quite honored. I'm looking forward to hearing her story.

Bernie slightly inclined her head, *It looks like we're going to get the chance. Shelley's heading back, and if I'm not mistaken, Mkali's mom is with him.*

Shelley and a stately woman, who looked like an adult version of Mkali, approached us. I noticed the slight upturn of her lips as she stifled the smile that sprang to her face when she saw her daughter and the way she was standing guard with Bernie.

"Your Majesty," she bowed low, "Sir Arktos said you would like my daughter to join you for refreshments in your tent. May I ask why?"

"Because she wishes to *Protect the Weak* and I would like to hear why she is so passionate regarding this at her young age. If you give your permission to have her join us for an hour or so, that is," I answered her with a bright smile.

"Of course, Sire," she answered. "I am sure Mkali will be on her best behavior and not eat too many sweets before dinner."

"Yes, Mama," Mkali answered while continuing to watch for threats.

I laughed. "We'll be fine, but I'll have to talk to my mom about spoiling her dinner. She tends to bake pies to help her relax so I'm sure she has plenty to share. Please tell me your name."

The woman's cheeks darkened in a blush. "My name is Shujaa, my husband is Askari and our family name is Kentauro."

"Well, Shujaa Kentauro, I would like to invite your daughter, Mkali, to join us for refreshments so she can tell us her story. I would also like to invite you and your husband to join us for dinner as well. Would that be agreeable to you?"

"We would be honored, Sire," Shujaa answered with a deep bow.

I stepped closer to Shujaa and clasped her hand in mine. "The honor is actually mine. I remember now that your husband is Quartermaster for General Arktos and he used to spend time answering the questions of an inquisitive dragon when I was younger. Sir Einhorn will bring Mkali home a little later and then will escort you all back when it's time for dinner."

"Thank you," Shujaa responded and nodded to her daughter. "Mkali, I will see you later, conduct yourself with honor."

"Yes, Mama," Mkali answered.

"Sir Einhorn, Mkali, would you please lead the way? I don't know about you two, but I could use some pie." I said and waved them forward, smiling at Shujaa as we walked past.

"I thought you said you were stuffed," Shelley whispered as we walked up the hill together.

"There's always room for Mom's pie," I answered.

"I couldn't agree more," Shelley replied.

"Would you like another piece of pie, Mkali?" Mom asked.

"No, thank you, Lady Drake," Mkali answered, "I don't want to spoil my dinner."

"I don't either," Shelley said, "so, I'll only have one more piece."

Bernie poked Shelley in the stomach but was met with rock hard muscle. "I'm still getting used to the less-squishy Shelley," she laughed.

I interrupted their banter before they could really get going. "So,

Mkali, please tell us why you are so determined to *Protect the Weak* at your age."

Mkali sighed before she began. "I was born on Earth, but my parents always told me stories of where we came from. They also taught me what it means to be a shifter from Theria who is loyal to the King."

"What type of shifter are you?" Bernie asked.

"I'm a centaur," Mkali answered with pride in her voice.

"I'm a unicorn, so it's almost like we're related," Bernie said with a grin which Mkali matched.

"Please continue your story," I gently prodded.

"When my parents came through the gate with everyone from the palace, they knew it would be years before they could go back to Theria so they wanted to make Earth their home. They were lucky that they could pass for humans and started a horse ranch."

"I always wanted to have a horse when I was a little girl," Bernie smiled.

"It turns out you were kind of a horse when you were a little girl," Shelley laughed.

Bernie tried to keep a straight face, but she smiled at Shelley's comment.

Mkali giggled. "That's funny since you're a unicorn."

"Yes, but I didn't know that when I was your age. What happened after your parents started the ranch?" Bernie asked.

"They were happy for a few years until the ranch got bigger and other ranchers in the area got jealous and started causing problems. At first they just talked bad about my parents but then started doing more stuff to hurt their business. Mama got pregnant with me around the same time and had to stay in her centaur form until after I was born. Baba had to tell people that Mama went to visit relatives because she was pregnant. It was hard for them to keep Mama hidden because their enemies kept saying Baba was mistreating the horses and inspectors kept coming to check.

"I asked why those people were so hateful and my parents told me that some of the other ranchers didn't like the color of our skin and were jealous of their success with horses. Baba said it got worse again when some of the others started telling people that my parents were in the country illegally and were connected to terrorists in Africa. Some of the businesses in the closest town stopped selling to my parents and since Baba wasn't willing to leave Mama alone for very long he couldn't drive to another town to get supplies. It was more expensive to have supplies shipped in so things got worse while Mama was pregnant." Mkali paused and wiped angry tears from her eyes with the back of her hand.

Bernie sat next to Mkali, put her arm around her small shoulders and gave her a squeeze. "You don't have to keep telling your story if you want to stop."

Mkali shook her head once and she narrowed her eyes as she continued to think through the things her parents had told her.

She continued. "Things almost turned deadly the night I was born. Mama had gone into labor and was in the barn when some men in masks came to burn my parents out. Baba was going to kill the men who had come to hurt us but some of our closest neighbors had heard about what was going on and stood in the way of the bad men.

"Even though their faces were covered, everyone knew who these people were. They finally backed down after shouting insults and threats at Baba and everyone who stood with him. After the bad men left, our neighbors promised to help keep watch to make sure the men didn't return. After I was born, my parents had to keep me hidden until I was able to shift into my human form. When I did, Mama and I appeared again and Baba told everyone we had come back from visiting our relatives.

"Our neighbors kept helping us and would often camp out on our ranch to make sure the bad people stayed away. It took months for things to finally die down but by that time, my parents had contacted a wolf shifter, who was also a lawyer, and got paperwork for us showing we were in the country legally. The physical attacks stopped but none of the local businesses would sell anything to my parents or to the neighbors who stood with us.

"I grew up watching the injustice that was handed out to people whose only crime was loving their neighbor. The people who were kind to my family suffered at the hands of hateful people who used their power to harm others. When I was five and started school, my friends and I were picked on and made fun of for how we looked because the adults had taught their children to be cruel. When other children would physically attack me and my friends, I would get into trouble for defending us. Mama finally started school at our house where my friends and I could learn in peace.

"When Mama and Baba told me that there was a King again and we would be going through the gate, I was so excited. But, I was also sad because we wouldn't be there to protect my friends and their families from the mean people. My parents arranged to buy each of our neighbor's ranches for a lot of money so they could start somewhere fresh because they knew it wouldn't be safe for them once we left. I was sad that we couldn't do more but we were leaving Earth. I promised myself that I would always follow the ways of the King and *Protect the Weak* whenever I had a chance."

Mkali looked so fierce as she told her story, but I could tell she had been hurt by the casual cruelty she had to face her entire life. I was moved by the bravery of this little centaur and wanted to honor what she had already done to *Protect the Weak.* While Mom hugged her and Shelley and Bernie told her how brave she had been I decided to contact my counselors.

Fritz, Stavros, I sent, *I need advice.*

Of course, Sire, Fritz sent.

You have but to ask, Stavros, replied.

I wish to honor Mkali Kentauro and her family for the trials they had to face while they were on Earth. Mkali has already shown she has a fierce sense of justice and has gone out of her way to protect those weaker than herself. I find this admirable for an eight-year-old. She already asked if she could go with us on our journey so she can fight injustice.

She has the heart of a warrior, just like her parents, Stavros sent.

A moment later Fritz added, *here's what I recommend you do…*

After I finished my silent conversation, we continued to ask Mkali questions about her life on Earth and truly enjoyed each other's company. Mom left us alone because she wanted to make sure dinner was ready in time for our guests' arrival. After an hour Frieda Einhorn came into the tent and informed Mkali that she would return her to her parents, but they would need to get some special clothing first. Before Mkali left, I once again got down on one knee and gave her a hug. She told me she was surprised I would lower myself to do something like that but realized what she had said and got embarrassed.

"Don't worry Mkali," Bernie said, "King Alister likes to do things to surprise people."

"Yep," I agreed, "and don't tell them, but I have a big surprise for your parents after dinner."

Mkali nodded and looked stunned as Frieda led her out of the tent.

"I know that look," Shelley accused, "you're up to something."

"Yep," I nodded.

"And you're not going to tell us what it is?" Bernie asked.

"Nope," I shook my head.

"Well, you're just a fountain of information, aren't you?" Shelley grunted.

"Of course," I laughed, "now get out of here until dinner, I've got things to do."

Mom and Miriam did a great job on the impromptu feast. They prepared a roast bayak which was tender and flavorful. They served a mashed vegetable dish the locals call eawish, which tastes like a cross between a radish and potato. This was accompanied by a green salad, fresh bread and of course pie. The food was delicious and our mealtime was filled with laughter and stories from the Kentauros regarding their time on Earth. Mkali was in awe as she sat between Bernie and Shelley and we all kept looking at her each time one of her parents would recount another tale of a time she stood up for someone who needed protection. Askari and Shujaa also gave more detail concerning the troubles they faced while they lived on Earth. I realized how fortunate I was to grow up with people who had served my father and mother and loved me like a son. I was also blessed that my two best friends were always with me as well. Not everyone had it as easy and I was finding out more about the prejudice and bigotry some of my people had faced while living on Earth.

Occasionally, I noticed Shujaa looking at her daughter in amazement. Not only had Frieda found a red and purple velvet dress in Mkali's size, she had also done something to tame her wild hair to keep it out of her face. Mkali became more comfortable with her seatmates as the night went on and a few times I heard her tease Shelley about something he said.

It was getting late, and we were going to start out for Eutheria the next day, but there was one important thing I wanted to do before we wrapped up dinner.

I cleared my throat. "I hate to break up the festivities, but we have a long journey ahead of us tomorrow."

"Yeah, around eight hundred miles, oof," Shelley's complaint was cut off by the sound of Bernie's hand hitting him in the chest and Mkali's giggles.

"As I was saying before being so rudely interrupted, we have a long journey tomorrow, so we need to wrap things up. Before we go, there is something important I want to do. Please bring everything inside," I said, raising my voice.

Two bear shifters in their human forms walked in carrying a large chair while being followed by two fox shifters carrying a large chest. Once they set their burdens down, I thanked them and they left the tent. Rising from the table I made my way over to the chair and sat. I nodded to Bernie and Shelley and they joined me to stand to the right and left of my chair.

"Mkali, would you please join us?" I asked. "Fritz, please show Miss Kentauro where to stand."

The adults stood from the table and Fritz led a stunned Mkali to stand five feet away from where I was sitting. Askari and Shujaa stood on her right, holding hands tightly.

I looked at a solemn Mkali and smiled before I began. "Mkali, you impressed me today when you stood blocking the path and asking if you could come with us on our journey." Shujaa gasped at my statement and I couldn't help laughing. "I began to admire you when you told me that you wanted to go so you could *Protect the Weak*. That admiration has turned to respect as I heard more of your story and how you embody the principles of the Kingdom of Theria even though you have never been there. Your parents named you Mkali which means fierce. You definitely live up to your name. You are fierce in spirit, fierce in honor and have the heart of a warrior."

I looked into Mkali's eyes as I continued, "Mkali Kentauro, do you acknowledge me as your King and pledge to serve me in whatever way I ask?"

"I do, Sire," Mkali answered.

"You asked me earlier today if you could come with me on our journey, and while I applaud your fierce determination, you cannot come yet because you aren't old enough to go on such a long journey without your parents and we don't have room to bring them too. Do you understand this?"

Mkali nodded her head and a tear of frustration streaked down her cheek, "Yes, Sire," she whispered.

"I know you're disappointed, but sometimes we're disappointed when we do the right thing. However, you won't always be eight years old and I have something for you to do now."

Bernie and Shelley, please get the items in the chest and put them on Mkali, I sent and they nodded.

They removed the items from the chest and approached Mkali. Bernie slipped the breastplate over Mkali's head and settled it on her shoulders. She fastened the buckles along the right side and stepped back. Shelley handed Bernie a sword in a scabbard and she belted it around Mkali's waist. The breastplate had been created for Mkali and fit her perfectly. My heraldic coat of arms, a crimson dragon in flight against a dark green background, was displayed on the front of the breastplate. Shelley draped a crimson cloak over her shoulders and fastened it with a clasp in the shape of a dragon. Both of my Knights returned to their places on either side of me. I heard a sob from Shujaa, but could see nothing but pride shining in her eyes. Mkali looked stunned.

"Earlier today Sir Einhorn warned you against putting your hand on a weapon in my presence, but we're going to make an exception," I winked at her. "Please draw your sword and hand it to me hilt first."

Mkali smoothly drew her sword and looked at the blade for a bit before she handed it to me hilt first.

"Please kneel," I said and stood from my chair, "Mkali Kentauro, centaur and daughter who brings delight and honor to her parents, I name you Fierceheart, Squire to Sir Einhorn and charge you to protect those weaker than yourself until we return."

I tapped her with the flat of the sword on her right shoulder, raised the sword over her head and tapped her on the left shoulder as well. I was grateful that Fritz had spent some time with me before dinner to show me what to do. I would hate to mess up such a solemn occasion.

"Please rise," I instructed her.

Mkali stood and I handed back her sword which she slid into the scabbard hanging from her belt. Taking a knee once again so I could look her in the eyes, I placed both of my hands on her shoulders and addressed her.

"When we return you will begin training with Sir Einhorn to prepare to one day join my court as one of my Knights. I'm not saying you can never join us on a journey to take out an enemy, I'm just telling you, you can't come yet. Do you understand?" I asked.

"Yes, thank you, Sire," Mkali answered.

"You're welcome, but I'm really thanking you for your faithfulness to the principles we all hold dear. I am proud of who you are and look forward to seeing who you will become."

Mkali leapt at me and hugged me as hard as she could. I looked over at her parents and saw they were beaming with love and pride as the others in the room were congratulating them and patting them on the back. I just kept thinking about this little girl who was holding me tightly and how she protected others when she was being treated horribly at the same time. I would do anything for Mkali and others like her who wanted to spend their lives trying to help others.

Son, your parents would be proud of you and how you are leading our people, Dad sent, *your mom and I are proud of you as well. You already have the loyalty of our people because you are King, but you are winning their hearts as well. Mkali represents those who will follow you for who you are and not just because your father and mother were beloved rulers. Each of us in here follows you for the same reasons.*

Thanks, Dad, that means a lot, I sent, *I'm kind of making this up as I go along.*

Dad's laughter came through our connection. *You've already learned one of the secrets of being an adult, we're mostly making this up as we go along, too.*

We dropped our mental connection and I smiled at the celebration going on in the room. Mkali was busy showing her sword to her parents and telling them how she felt during the ceremony. I was looking at Askari and our eyes met, *thank you,* he mouthed to me and I bowed to him. My heart swelled as I looked around the room at my friends and family and how they had welcomed Mkali and her parents into our group. They were now part of this extended family whether they knew it or not.

CHAPTER FIVE

Kingdom of Theria
Royal Palace Overlook

Dimitri could see the purple sheen of the shield covering the palace. Even though his scholars and scientists had been working for over thirteen years to take down the shield, they were no closer today than they were when they first started. He ground his teeth in frustration. He had plotted and planned so carefully. If Phillip and Beatrice would've died after drinking the poison like they were supposed to, he would now be sitting on the throne. But they hadn't. He had to give Phillip credit, he had always been stubborn and even in defeat, he refused to die. Well, no matter, even a mighty Royal Dragon has to eat and drink. At most, Phillip and Beatrice could last a few months more, and then he was sure the shield would fall.

He looked to the west and could see his army camped on the arrival meadow. They were arrayed facing the most likely location where a gate would be created if that traitorous scientist were correct and there actually had been gate activity on Claw. It was a pity he couldn't question the scientist for himself, it was even more of a pity that he couldn't kill Weston again for his incompetence. Still, it didn't hurt to be prepared and his army was ready for a fight.

It was strangely quiet in this part of the kingdom because all the shifters were gone. Either they had escaped through the gate to Claw with Gustav and the rest of his former friends or they had fled to other parts of the kingdom. At first, he hadn't bothered to chase them because he was convinced he would quickly take over the palace. However, after months of failure getting into the palace, he finally decided to round up the missing shifters, only to discover his scouts were unable to find any signs of where they had gone. Each time he sent out a patrol to locate missing shifters only a few would return. After losing over a hundred men to the traitors, he made the decision to return to his fortress in the north and leave a brigade to handle any stragglers they found.

The more he thought through the failures and setbacks he experienced since he sprung his trap, the angrier he became. There was no way a comatose dragon would defeat him. He would dance on Phillip's corpse once he succumbed to a lack of food and water. He wouldn't dance on Beatrice's corpse, but he would pick her body apart to create weapons he could use to conquer any who would think to stand against him. And if the hatchling, Alister, showed up after he had the weapons, it would be rather poetic to kill him with something that had been a part of his mother. It would serve her right for choosing Phillip over him.

Envisioning the deaths of his former friends and their child soothed his anger and helped calm him. He took a deep breath and looked again at the palace and surrounding countryside. It really was quite beautiful here, but once he had access to the palace, he would destroy everything as far as the eye could see, then salt the ground so nothing could ever grow there again. He couldn't allow anything to stand to remind people of the former King and Queen.

He would wait. He would ready his army and would personally kill the hatchling. He allowed himself a smile as he thought of standing over the lifeless bodies of his opponents. He knew it was his destiny to rule, he just had to take care of a few minor annoyances first. Dimitri sighed and began humming a happy little tune as he thought of the death and destruction that would soon commence.

Middle Earth

When we took off, I thought the hardest part of travel would be the physical strain of flying eight hours a day. But it was actually the mind-numbing boredom that came from flying so many miles at a time. At first, it was amazing to see the changes in landscape and the different animals we could see from the air but even that grew tedious the longer we flew.

The first few hours of travel were filled with the joy and thrill that came from doing something we never thought possible. We laughed, shared stories and pointed out amazing sights to each other. Even though we took a break after our first four hours of travel, we were so exhausted at the end of the day we could barely make camp. Those of us who flew were wiped out, but our passengers were as well. Thankfully we had enough food with us that we didn't have to hunt the first night; none of us could have pulled that off.

We were physically healed by the time we set off on day two, but none of us were thrilled to get going again. We flew fairly close to the ground but there were a few times we had to climb higher to clear mountains in our path. It took more of our energy to climb to higher elevations and our passengers were miserable because of the cold. Those of us who could breathe fire were able to heat the air around our passengers but Gustav wasn't able to do that, so Wu had to partially shift to cover his body in fur. It made it more difficult for Gustav to fly and for Wu to hang on.

By the end of day two, all our nerves were frayed and tempers were short. We needed fresh meat, so Mom and I decided to go hunting rather than stay in camp to watch people we loved gripe at one another. We were able to capture some animals that looked like moose, but approximately twice the size of the ones on Earth. I didn't know what they were called, and I didn't really care, I just knew they were delicious. Mom and I felt better after we ate our fill but we didn't return right away.

Alister, I know we want to get to Eutheria as rapidly as we can but I'm wondering if we should slow down a bit, Mom sent.

I've been thinking the same thing but feel like time is running out to save my parents. I've been having the same dream and receiving the same warning that I need to find them, but my father's voice is getting a little softer each night.

Mom sighed mentally as she answered me, *Honey, I understand, but let's talk to the others to see what they have to say, okay?*

That's probably for the best. Can you carry two of these animals back to camp? I'll grab three and meet you there. I need to spend some time alone.

Sure honey, Mom sent and took off to camp.

I shifted into my human form, sat on a nearby log and pushed my senses outward to make sure I wouldn't be surprised by a hungry predator. Even though I try to be neat when I eat my meals, it's kind of messy to eat as a dragon and nothing draws predators faster than the smell of fresh blood.

Sitting there, I pondered what we were trying to do. Was I being foolish by pushing everyone so hard to rush to Eutheria just to find my parents were already dead? What if my brain were playing tricks on me and I was hoping for the impossible? I chuckled to myself because I was already living the impossible; I was a dragon and came from a dimension filled with shifters. Listening to the quiet surrounding me, I continued to think about what it would mean if we conquered Dimitri and my parents were already dead.

Nothing...I concluded that it wouldn't change anything. Dimitri had committed treason by plotting to kill the King and Queen, he wrongfully imprisoned families in order to force good people to do evil. We didn't have any idea what he had been doing since we escaped to Earth, but if he continued the way he had before we left, he'd multiplied his crimes for over thirteen years. The mantle of my rule settled heavily on my shoulders as I realized that we needed to stop Dimitri as swiftly as possible without putting others in needless danger. We were exhausted; there were thousands of miles ahead of us, but we would press on. Our goal, our focus must be to free the Kingdom of Theria from the tyranny of Dimitri as soon as we could. If I could find my parents still alive, after we destroyed Dimitri, that would be a blessing. But even if they were dead, we would press on as planned. With that settled in my mind, I headed back to camp.

The sun was still in the sky when I returned. We were so far north the sun didn't completely set at this time of year so I could easily see the dark clouds racing in our direction. I was buffeted by strong winds and lightning flashed in the distance. We were in for a storm. Great! As I got closer to our camp I could see Bernie and her parents in their unicorn form, grazing on the lush grass. Shelley was watching over them as they ate.

I smiled to myself as I sent to him, *Dude, you have it bad for Bernie, don't you?*

Yeah, I do, he sent, I could see the goofy smile on his face as he answered me.

You do know she and her parents can take care of themselves if anything attacks, right?

I know, but it makes me feel better when I can keep an eye on them as well. Besides, I asked Bernie if it was okay and she told me it makes her feel safer when I watch over her.

That's cool, dude. I've got dinner, hope you're hungry.

*I'm so hungry I could eat a horse...*Shelley immediately stopped because he realized what he was saying, *not that I would ever really eat a horse, I mean horses must be related to unicorns, right? I'd never do that, I just meant—you know what? Never mind.*

I laughed so hard, I snorted fire. I dropped the carcasses of the three animals I had brought back near the tent.

"Dragon delivery," I said after transforming.

Hey dude, Shelley sent, *let's not mention the horse comment to Bernie, like ever, okay?*

I've got your back, bro, I sent and walked toward the nearby lake to wash up.

After dinner, we sat around the fire with full bellies, enjoying the moment of quiet. I didn't want to break the mood but figured we needed to discuss our travel plans and whether we would slow down.

"Everyone is exhausted already and we've only been traveling for two days. My mom and I were talking earlier and she thought we might want to slow down. What do the rest of you think?" I asked.

"Over the last two days, I have never flown so far or so fast in my life," Gustav said, "and I am not ashamed to admit I was having trouble keeping up the last hour today."

"I'm not having trouble keeping pace, but am concerned about our passengers," Dad said tiredly.

"We bears are made to endure," Miriam added, "however, I didn't realize how tiring it would be to be a passenger. While I wouldn't mind slowing down, we will have to cover these miles eventually. I already want to get this trip over with so I say we keep to our plan."

Frieda spoke up next. "Unicorns are not really used to being passengers, we're more used to carrying others than being carried ourselves. I would like to slow down."

I noticed both Stavros and Fritz nodding in agreement as their wives spoke. I looked at Wu and encouraged him to speak. "What's your opinion, Wu?"

Wu bowed from his seated position and answered, "I do not believe I should express an opinion on this matter."

"Why is that?" I asked curiously.

"Firstly, I haven't earned the right to have a say in our travel plans. Secondly, as King, you are the one who makes the final decision. I will obey the choice you make and follow without complaint."

"Thank you, Wu, but, I need wise people to advise me in order to make the best decisions. I would like your input."

"Very well," Wu agreed. "We need to get to Eutheria as quickly as possible. Every instant we wait is another opportunity for Dimitri to work his evil."

"Thank you. Bernie, Shelley, you've been awfully quiet, what do you think?"

"I think we maintain our pace," Bernie answered matter-of-factly.

Shelley looked at everyone else before he stared straight at me to give his answer, "I've had a horrible attitude today because I was focused on my own comfort. To be honest, my butt hurts from riding so many hours. I don't do well with inaction or feeling that I'm not being useful. When I looked at Gustav, Albert, Fiona and Alister and thought about all the effort it's taking them to carry us so far, my attitude got worse. Rather than encourage Alister or any of the rest of you, I decided to sit and sulk. I'm ashamed of my attitude. Alister, I think we need to get there as speedily as we can. I'm not going to complain anymore, and I'll do everything I can to help."

"Thank you, Shelley, I've missed your horsing around," I said with a mischievous smile as the color drained from his face. "Mom, what do you think?" I asked.

"You told me earlier that you were feeling a sense of urgency, and it may be possible your parents were still alive. I lost hope a long time ago because I believed that Phillip and Beatrice were dead. If there is even a remote chance that your dreams are true, we need to find out as soon as we can. It has been so long since I've been so physically exhausted that I've forgotten what I'm capable of, what we're all capable of. We must keep going, we owe it to you to make sure."

I sat quietly for a long moment to consider everyone's advice before making my decision.

"Thank you for your counsel. I hope and pray that my parents are still alive and we can save them. This is a possibility and enough reason for me to keep going. However, the one thing I know for certain is Dimitri must be stopped and the longer it takes us to get to Theria, the more time he has to hurt our people. We will stop when we need to, we will rest when we need to, but we will push ourselves as much as we can so we can open a gate to Eutheria as swiftly as possible. Are we in agreement?" I asked and looked at each person as they nodded.

"Very well, let's try to get at least eight hours sleep." I looked up at the sky. "At least the storm clouds are blocking the sun, so it isn't as bright as it was before."

"Maybe we'll get some rain," Shelley said cheerfully.

Bernie elbowed him in the side, "I think I liked you better when you grumbled," she teased.

We stopped laughing as the rain began pouring from the sky.

Opening my eyes I was surprised to see a field of flowers instead of the camp where I fell asleep. Taking a deep breath I was overwhelmed by the scents coming from the flowers. I tried to categorize what I was smelling and discovered these were scents I had never smelled before. There were also colors I couldn't identify, and each flower seemed to glow with a life of its own. I stood, stretched my wings and looked around to see if I could figure out where I was. There weren't any trees and the field of flowers seemed to go on forever in every direction. I sat on my haunches when I realized this was a dream. At least it was a different dream than the one I had been having every night for weeks.

All my anxiety faded away as I was cocooned in peace. I started to lay down again to enjoy the warmth of the sun on my back when there was a faint sound behind me. Standing again, I turned and saw a lion coming towards me. Even though he was still quite some distance from me I could tell he was huge and could feel the ground tremble slightly with each step he took. His beautiful, golden fur softly reflected the sunlight and I could hear the rumble of a purr coming from his chest. I stood transfixed as he approached, his eyes twinkling with humor.

I was shocked when I realized he was larger than me. I looked down at myself to make sure I was still in my dragon form, because the lion made me feel so small. The lion laughed and the sound vibrated through my entire body with the deep richness of his voice. The laughter swelled outward from where he stood and it seemed as though the flowers were basking in the sound emanating from this magnificent beast.

"Are you Aslan?" I asked, surprised that the question came from my mouth rather than from my thoughts.

The lion smiled at me as he answered, "I am the First, I am the One, I am the Creator—but, Aslan works fine if that's easier for you." He winked at me.

"Where am I?" I asked.

"You are still where you were when you went to sleep," the lion grinned, "but you are dreaming of a location in my kingdom."

I looked at everything around me in amazement. "This is unbelievable," I breathed.

Once again the lion laughed and this time I found myself laughing with him. "Oh, Alister, I do appreciate the way you make me laugh. When you were back on Earth, you would have thought it unbelievable that you were a dragon and King of Theria. How easily you've adjusted to that idea. This is just one more thing you will learn to accept in time."

I nodded in acceptance, "It is nice to dream about something different than I have been, but why am I here?"

"I wanted to talk to you in a way your mind would accept and thought it would be easier for me to take this form and meet you in this place. Please walk with me," he said as he walked past me.

We walked together in silence for a bit and as I looked at him out of the corner of my eye I wondered whether he had grown or I had gotten smaller.

"Both are correct," the lion answered my musings, "the more time you spend with me, the larger I become, and you become a bit smaller in your own sight at the same time. Alister, do you know why dragons rule Theria?"

"Because they were willing to use their strength to unite the other kingdoms under their rule," I answered.

The lion shook his head. "It's actually because they were willing to use their strength and power to serve others rather than take what they wanted by force. Alister, your ancestor, Milleadh, asked me for help because the rule of the strongest was slowly killing shifters. If something hadn't changed when Milleadh asked me for help, the shifters on Theria would have been killed off in another hundred years or so."

"What happened?"

"I came to Milleadh, in a place similar to this and told him he could continue on as he had and dominate his people, or he could choose my way and I would teach him how to serve his people instead. This was the same offer I have made to every other Royal Dragon before Milleadh, but they had rejected my way for the path of dominance.

Milleadh was a mighty warrior, and by himself had defeated entire armies in battle. He had already killed the last Royal Dragon who challenged him and he thought there wasn't anyone else who could harm him. He was a prideful dragon and for a while, it looked like he would reject me as well. Fortunately, he had recently found his true mate in a dragon named Síocháin and he truly loved her and wanted a different life for his mate. He also wanted a different life for his child who was developing in the egg his mate had recently laid.

"Milleadh and I spoke for weeks as I answered each of his questions. He chose to bow his knee to me, asked for my help and swore to follow a different path. Milleadh didn't know that I had already been talking with Síocháin and she had asked me to intervene in her mate's life if possible. After Milleadh swore to me, I changed his name to Dóchas because his decision to choose a different path brought hope to all the shifters of Theria. He was true to his word and with Síocháin by his side they changed Theria."

"Why are you telling me this?" I asked.

"This is something your parents would have taught you if they had been able to. This is knowledge that is only known to Royal Dragons and is usually passed from parent to child at the right time. I have come to each Royal Dragon in turn over the millennia to give them this same choice, now it's your turn." I stopped walking as the lion moved in my way and turned to face me.

"Alister Rex, you have two paths before you. One path is based on ruling your people with the strength inherent to a Royal Dragon. If you follow this path you will defeat your enemies with the power you hold because of what you are. The second path is based on a choice to follow my ways and serve your people with the strength and power given to you to *Protect the Weak.* Which path do you choose?"

I was going to choose the path of serving immediately but began to think about what it would be like to command everyone to obey me. They would have to because I was more powerful and they couldn't stand against me. It would be so easy for me to open a gate into Theria and slip through by myself. I imagined what it would be like to attack Dimitri and his armies from the sky and how soundly they would be defeated. Some innocents might die but I would be able to end the battle without my friends getting hurt.

And yet, my musings were interrupted by a memory of my parents when I was five years old, before they flew off to meet Dimitri. We were standing on top of the palace and my mother told me how a wise ruler serves the people in their care. Some of her last words to me were *Protect the Weak*. I thought of the examples set by my birth parents, my adopted parents and those who chose to follow me. Lastly, I thought of an eight-year-old girl named Mkali who stood up for others who were weaker than herself and made my decision.

"I choose to follow you," I said and bowed low before the lion.

"I knew you would," he said as he lay his heavy paw on my head, "Phillip and Beatrice would be proud."

Standing with a stronger sense of purpose and resolve, I knew I'd made the right choice. If I had chosen to take the path of power, I would've been nothing more than a bully by forcing people to follow me.

"And that would be a problem for you because you hate bullies," the lion chuckled.

"What would've happened if I'd chosen to go my own way?" I asked.

"I would have removed your ability to connect to shifters. That ability to connect is special because not only do you gain strength from that connection but, you have the ability to guide others through it as well."

"You mean like mind control?" I wondered.

"No, nothing like that, it's more like influencing others to follow your example. For instance, if you were connected to everyone and chose to go your own way, you would influence others towards selfishness and a lack of concern for others. People could still overcome that, but your influence would be powerful and not something I want others to experience. However, since you chose to follow me, you will influence others to follow my path, serving others and accepting those who are different."

"But I felt the connection when I fought Minos. What if I'd acted selfishly before I chose you?" I asked.

"I wasn't worried because each set of parents, birth and adopted, have taught you my ways since you were young. You have been following me through their example your entire life, but it was time for you to choose for yourself. However, I know you, Alister, I know your heart and what drives you. I knew you would choose me."

I stood transfixed and thought about everything he had told me and realized who I was really talking to. "Thank you An'Ceann, it is an honor to meet you."

An'Ceann chuckled with a twinkle in his eye. "You figured it out; for a while I thought I hadn't given you enough hints," he said with a smile.

"Well, in my defense I thought this was just a dream when we started talking."

"It's been great visiting with you, Alister, but it's time you woke up. You have a long way to go and much to do."

"Will you answer one question for me?" I asked.

The look of kindness he gave me as he shook his head rocked me, "I'm sorry Alister, I won't answer that for you. You'll have to find out for yourself. But I do want you to know that I'm here for you, even if you can't see me, no matter what happens," he said as he faded away.

I laid on the ground and closed my eyes. It felt like I was enveloped in a warm embrace before drifting off to sleep.

I awoke to the sound of rain pouring around me and cracked my eye open. Yep, it was still raining and I was lying on the ground. I could sense my friends and family sleeping close to my body as I kept them warm and dry. It felt good to know I could use my wings and body to provide a shield against the elements for the people I loved. Laughing to myself I thought of the new nicknames Shelley could come up for me, like, Umbrella, Raincoat or Slicker. It didn't bother me, in fact, his nicknames helped me stay grounded.

I checked the *Dies* spell I cast before going to sleep and was surprised to discover I had only been asleep for an hour. As I settled back down to finish my rest, I contemplated everything An'Ceann had told me and was amazed that he actually came to me in my dream. Unfortunately, I couldn't share my experience or the things he told me with anyone other than a Royal Dragon. As I fell back to sleep I was thinking about how I hoped to meet another one someday.

Even though it rained off and on the whole day as we flew across what was Nunavut, Canada and Greenland on Earth, we still were in good spirits when we stopped for the night. We had covered over eight hundred miles during the day and we were adjusting to so many hours of travel. Along the way, we took the time to appreciate the beauty of the countryside below us and notice more animals that were similar to those on Earth. There were vast herds of wooly mammoths, but they were easily three times as large as any that had ever walked on Earth.

Shelley really wanted me to fly close to some animals that looked like polar bears because he wanted to test his strength against them. Bernie argued against that because she didn't want him to hurt such a magnificent creature for sport. When we were over the ocean heading for the landmass that corresponded to Greenland, we could see huge sea serpents frolicking in the water and hunting a pod of animals that looked like whales. We flew over them too swiftly to see what happened, but it looked like the serpents were going to eat whale for dinner.

I was a bit concerned at one point when we were over the ocean because there were bolts of lightning shooting from the sky a few miles to the south of us. I certainly didn't want to find out how much it hurt to be struck by lightning and neither did my passengers.

Hey everyone, I broadcast, *what do you think we should do to avoid the lightning?*

The static electricity is making my hair stand on end, Bernie added.

Wait, wait, Shelley said excitedly, *let me see if I can send you a mental picture of what she looks like.*

There was a little bit of silence before Miriam sent, *Stavros, do you think we should help Sheldon out here?*

Help me with what? Shelley asked, *Do you know how to send a mental picture?*

I think this is something he'll have to learn the hard way, Stavros groaned while the rest of the adults chuckled.

Oookay—I continued, *what should we do about the storm?*

I don't think we need to worry right now, we've passed the worst of the lightning and it is already many miles behind us, Gustav answered.

Well, that's good, I sighed, *I really didn't want to get struck by lightning.*

It sort of tickles, Mom sent, *although it wouldn't be any fun for our passengers.*

Remember the electrical storm we flew through after we were married? Dad asked.

Yes, I do, Mom purred, *and then…*

Wait, I interrupted *if you two are going to take a walk down memory lane, can you at least switch to a private channel? TMI about my parents is wrong whether I'm human or dragon.*

All the adults laughed at that comment as well.

I figured it out, Shelley shared mentally across our connection.

*You might not want to...*Frieda tried to interrupt Shelley.

You're going to love this, Shelley crowed as he sent us a mental picture of Bernie's hair sticking up. In the picture, Bernie must have been glaring at Shelley and she held her right index finger up in warning. Her blonde hair was sticking up from her head like a halo and she was trying to smooth it back down with her left hand.

Shelley's bellowing laugh could be heard over the wind, but so could the sound of a hand slapping an arm.

Ow, Shelley sent, *what was that for?*

You have a lot to learn, Sheldon Petros Arktos. Don't you ever, and I mean ever send a picture of me looking so hideous to anyone else or you and I will have a sparring session you'll never forget, Bernie seethed.

Ah, c'mon Bernie, you always look beautiful to me, even if your hair looks like Medusa's.

Son, Stavros growled, *I advise you to stop talking, now, you're only making things worse.*

I'm sorry, Bernie, Shelley began, *I really—*

Private channel, I mentally yelled while laughing at Shelley's latest blunder, *and dude, if I were you, I'd let it go until we land so you can grovel properly.*

The rest of the day passed uneventfully and we were able to find a camping spot rather quickly. Bernie and Shelley headed off to the woods to gather firewood. Frieda and Miriam followed a hundred feet or so behind them. I think it was so Shelley wouldn't accidentally make things worse and Bernie would actually be willing to listen to Shelley's apology while he groveled.

"Ah, young love," Mom sighed as she watched the procession pass out of sight.

"I don't really understand what the big deal was. Shelley didn't mean to make Bernie look bad, and the picture was pretty funny," I said.

Mom looked at me for so long, I didn't think she was going to respond. Finally, she did, "Alister, you Shelley and Bernie have been friends for so long that you sometimes forget that Bernie is a young woman. You and Shelley can get away with teasing each other and point out when one of you does something goofy. No woman wants to be made to feel stupid, and that's what Shelley did when he sent the mental picture to the rest of us. It probably wouldn't have been a big deal if he just shared it with Bernie and you but by including everyone else, her feelings were hurt."

"Why didn't anyone warn him?" I asked.

"You know your friend, would he have listened?" Mom asked.

I thought for a few seconds before answering, "No, he wouldn't. Shelley doesn't have a mean bone in his body but when he thinks something's funny, he wants to share it with everyone else."

"You're probably right," Mom agreed, "but I think he learned a valuable lesson today and won't make that same mistake again."

"Do you think they'll be okay?" I asked worriedly.

"Oh sure," Mom laughed, "this is just something they're going to have to talk through. This won't be the last mistake Shelley makes, it's all part of the process of becoming more than friends. Sometimes young men stop thinking as clearly as they should when they're around beautiful young women." Mom put her arm around my shoulder as we moved towards the tent the others had set up.

"Well, I know one thing," I added, "I'm going to learn from Shelley and not make the same mistakes myself if I ever find my mate."

"Keep telling yourself that, son," Mom laughed. I heard the other adults within hearing distance chuckle as well. Maybe they knew something I didn't.

CHAPTER SIX

M*iddle Earth*

We finally reached our destination six days after departing the meadow where we left the rest of the shifters. It took us longer than expected because we rested a full day before attempting the almost six-hundred-mile trek over the ocean from Greenland to Iceland. We didn't have any difficulty flying over the ocean but we did have to make some course corrections as we neared Iceland because the volcanoes on Middle Earth are more active than they are on Earth. Our planned overnight camp was covered in lava.

The last two days of travel were mostly over the ocean, and there wasn't a lot to see. What we did see, all looked the same. Gustav taught us a spell called *Via* which helped us stay on course. As we flew, I decided to ask Gustav a question regarding some of the new words I had been using, especially those used for spells.

Gustav, are you able to answer some questions while we fly?

Laughing through our connection he replied, *If we were speaking out loud I wouldn't be able to but since I do not need to breathe while using thought-speech I can.*

Are you doing okay? I sent. *We've been flying for hours so far.*

I am fine, just not used to flying so long, especially with a passenger on my back. At least Wu and I have had some interesting discussions to help pass the time.

It's a good thing you had time to make him his own thought medallion before we started on our journey, I remarked.

Yes, he sent, *it would have made the journey more difficult for me if he couldn't have responded to my thoughts as easily as he can with a thought medallion.*

Not to mention it's great he can shift his clothes as well since he has been partially shifted the entire journey to help him keep warm, I laughed.

That is true, Gustav sent, *what is the question you want to ask? And is it just a question for me, or can everyone be part of the discussion?*

I was startled that I didn't think about including everyone, even though we had been using thought-speech exclusively for days, I sometimes forgot we could all communicate at the same time this way. Opening a channel to everyone, I sent, *Attention, ladies, and gentlemen, this is your captain speaking. As you can see we're still flying over the ocean and will be for a few more hours. If you look to your right, you will see the endless ocean. But, if you look to your left, you will see the ocean which is never-ending.* I could sense the humor coming from everyone in our group. *Just kidding, I have a question for Gustav and decided it would be good for everyone to weigh in.* After receiving agreement from everyone, I continued, *Gustav, why do all of the words we use for spells seem like they come from Latin?*

Because they do, Gustav answered, *or at least, Latin is one of the languages shifters taught the people in some of the dimensions we explored.*

Why Latin? I asked.

As you know, our race is very long-lived, Gustav explained, *and our scientists were very influential at various stages in human history. Many of the myths around Earth can be directly connected to encounters the humans had with various shifters over the millennia. At first, these encounters were one-sided. The shifters would show themselves in their true forms and then record what happened. Over time, these encounters weren't enough for our scientists so they looked for ways to communicate. In Eutheria, we had two languages most scientists used and these were close to languages some of the humans were already using. They developed into Greek and Latin.*

At least these are the languages that developed in Southern Europe, Wu broke in, *there were different languages developed in Asia and Africa. These languages were based on pictographs.*

Wait a minute, Shelley interrupted, *I remember hearing about pictographs from Mr. Schliebe—I mean Gustav—when we were in sixth grade. Weren't pictographs used in Sumer, Egypt and China?*

Very good, Sir Arktos, Gustav praised, *and I wasn't sure if you were paying attention in my class.*

To be honest, I only remember this because Alister and Bernie helped me study for the final exam on ancient civilizations, Shelley admitted.

I'm still impressed you remembered that after everything we've been through. Bernie agreed. I could sense Shelley swell with pride through our connection.

The same thing occurred among early human groups in almost every country on Earth. As you already know, Eutheria corresponds to Europe, Carnivoria to Africa, Sirenea to Asia, Theria to North America, Marsupia to Australia, Cetacea to Oceania and Metatheria to South America, Fritz added. *If humans at large knew the truth concerning shifters, many of their mysteries would be solved.*

What do you mean? I asked.

Sphinxes have an affinity for pyramids and we like to teach others how to build them, Gustav admitted.

Wow, Bernie breathed, *mind blown.*

Even though we had hours of light left when we finally landed in Scotland, we decided to set up camp and then do some hunting and exploring. The plan was for me to open the gate from Middle Earth to Theria early the next morning. We would then fly to the castle where

Mom grew up and where Moss was currently ruling Eutheria. Mom assured us that even though Moss was conceited, stubborn, prejudiced and craved recognition, he was loyal to the King of Theria and wouldn't cause us any problems. Mom actually used a lot more colorful language and there were a couple of times she snorted fire as she spoke. She was still angry at Moss for his treatment of Dad after they got married.

Once we had everything set up, I took Bernie and Shelley with me so we could explore the area to see if there were any settlements nearby. Everyone would be on the lookout for good hunting and share the location with each other in case game animals were scarce. Once I got back into the air, I realized we needn't have worried. There were thousands of animals that looked like a cross between a yak and a wildebeest grazing below us.

It is so weird to see all this open land but no people, Bernie sent.

Yeah, Shelley agreed, *there aren't a lot of people in Maine where we grew up, but it seems like there have never been any people living here.*

Let's find a place to land so we can eat and then hang out for a bit, I added.

I landed within sight of twenty of the hairy animals. I wasn't looking forward to dealing with fur between my teeth but I was hungry. The animals barely gave us a glance so it was evident they had never seen a dragon before. Bernie and Shelley slid off and turned into their animals.

I'm going to do some grazing, Bernie sent, *while you two carnivores get your dinner on.*

Be safe, Shelley sent as he and Bernie rubbed muzzles.

You too, Bernie sent, as she flicked him with her tail.

*Ummm...*I interrupted, *you do realize you're not on a private thought channel again, right?*

I didn't know a bear and unicorn could blush, so I learned something new. If possible, they got even more embarrassed as I laughed.

Don't worry, I sent, *I think you're cute.*

You really don't mind that we're dating? Bernie asked timidly.

We've already gone over this, I sent, *besides my parents told me I can only find a true mate in another Royal Dragon.*

Dude, Shelley added, *that's got to be rough for you.*

Not really, I sent back, *I've been a bit too busy to even think about things like that.*

Bernie and Shelley both looked at me so I relented, *Okay, I've thought about it; but there's too much to do for me to dwell on it. I'm hungry, so I'm off. Be careful!* I laughed in my mind as I flew away.

Flying far enough away from my friends so they wouldn't have to see me eat, I spotted my meal. I've gotten better at eating in my dragon form, but it's still a messy business. I killed five of the animals and roasted them with my fire. Usually, I eat my meals raw as a dragon, but didn't want to get hair between my teeth and the fire burned off all the hair. Yay, me!

Even though I knew Bernie and Shelley really wanted to know how I felt about their relationship I hadn't been completely honest with them. I'm glad they fell for each other and really hoped that they were true mates but couldn't help feeling a bit left out. It could take me decades before I ever met a female Royal Dragon and who knew how long it would take to find a true mate. Rather than dwell on something that couldn't be changed, I decided to finish eating and then rejoin Bernie and Shelley.

When I flew back to my friends they were sitting close together, in their human forms. I transformed and joined them on the lawn. We hadn't had much time to just hang out together since we started our journey. However, I must have been the topic of conversation because they quit talking when I got close. Shelley had a grin on his face but Bernie looked exasperated.

I decided to ignore them for a bit and lay back to watch the white clouds scuttle across the sky. Even though I couldn't see what was going on with my friends, I was pretty sure they were having a private conversation using thought-speak. Shelley continued to snicker and Bernie must have had enough because she burst out, "You want to know so badly, you ask him."

"Ha!" Shelley crowed, "you spoke first so you lost. You have to ask."

"But, I don't really care," Bernie retorted.

"I don't make the rules, just enforce them," Shelley chuckled.

"You know I can hear you, right?" I muttered. "What do you want to ask me?" I sat up and turned to face my friends.

Bernie looked embarrassed, but after sending a glare Shelley's way, she squared her shoulders and opened her mouth to speak; nothing came out.

"You can't use thought-speech to ask the question. The bet was, whoever talks first has to ask Alister, out loud," Shelley said as he crossed his arms.

"Fine, fine!" Bernie threw up her arms in defeat. "Alister, when you're a dragon and you eat like, five animals at a time, where does all that food go when you turn back to your human form?"

I was so surprised that it took me a little bit before answering, "I don't know, I've never thought about it before."

"Nice try, Bernie," Shelley said with a wicked gleam in his eye, "that's not the real question, and you know it."

"I'm so embarrassed," Bernie said as she palmed her face. "Alister, after you eat...I mean, after you eat as a dragon, how do you...where do you?"

Shelley laughed as he practically shouted, "Do you go poop as a dragon or a human to get rid of all the waste from all the food you eat?"

I must have been gaping like a fish on land and looked back and forth between my two friends. Shelley had a huge grin on his face Bernie had both hands over her face and her shoulders were shaking in laughter.

"Let me get this straight," I said when I finally managed to speak. "You could ask me anything you want relating to me being a dragon and the only thing you want to know is how I poop?"

I rolled my eyes as my two friends flopped back on the ground holding their sides, howling with laughter.

"No, no, we want to know more but that's what we want to know first," Bernie finally managed to gasp out.

"How did this even come up in conversation?" I wondered.

"Bernie and I were talking about how your scales looked so cool and then we started to wonder if all the dragon legends on Earth came from people actually seeing dragons from Theria," Shelley started.

"Then we discussed the coolest dragons from some of our favorite movies and we compared you to the ones in those," Bernie continued.

"FYI, we agreed that you're cooler than any of those in movies," Shelley added.

"Thank you, I guess," I muttered, "but, I'm still not sure how that leads to you asking about my bathroom habits."

"We're getting there," Shelley replied. "After we had the conversation regarding dragons, I mentioned how cool the T-Rex was from the first *Jurassic Park* movie—"

"And then we talked about some of our favorite scenes from it," Bernie said.

"And I brought up the scene where Ellie stuck her arm in the huge pile of triceratops poop."

"Of course you did," I said and closed my eyes.

"And then Shelley wondered if a pile of dragon poop was bigger than a pile of triceratops poop. That's how we got to the question concerning your, um, bathroom habits," Bernie said as she blushed.

"You two are so weird," I grinned. "So how did you get to the bet?"

"That's easy," Shelley replied glibly, "we argued about who would ask you the question and then made the bet whoever talks first would have to do it. Bernie was convinced I couldn't keep quiet longer than her so she was sure I was going to have to ask."

"I figured it was a safe bet, I just forgot that Shelley could taunt me in thought-speech before I caved in," Bernie admitted.

"And when did you have this conversation?" I wondered.

"Off and on for the past few days," Shelley shrugged. "This just felt like the best time to bring it up."

I shook my head at my friends' antics but was grateful to them for keeping things weird. "Thanks, guys, with you two around, I'll never take myself too seriously."

"We're here to help," Shelley answered and looked at me expectantly.

"What?" I asked.

"Aren't you going to answer the question?" He asked.

"Nope," I said cheerfully and laughed at the look of disappointment on their faces.

"But I will say this," I winked, "a triceratops has nothing on a dragon." We all laughed together.

We spent the next hour or so talking about inconsequential things and recounting highlights from our trip so far. I was laying on my back with my hands folded behind my head and Bernie and Shelley were laying on either side of me. We had lapsed into the type of silence that only good friends can achieve as they enjoy their time together.

Surprisingly, it was Bernie who once again spoke first. "What do you think we'll experience tomorrow when you create a gate above Eutheria?"

We had decided it would be safer for me to open a gate in the air and fly from Middle Earth to Theria rather than open a gate on the ground. We wanted to be extra careful in case Dimitri could find a point of weakness between dimensions and attack the people we'd left behind.

"I'm not sure," I answered. "I've only made gates on the ground before. I suppose I can make the gate obvious so we will know when we've flown through it but other than that, I'm not sure what to expect."

"I remember the sky there is darker than it is here, we'll probably notice that when the gate is open," Shelley mused.

"Once again, you surprise me with your attention to detail," I teased.

"I'll have you know, I've always paid attention to detail," Shelley huffed. "I'm just easily distracted—squirrel."

"We've noticed," Bernie said with a smile in her voice.

"Mom said we should come out ten miles, or so, from the castle in Eutheria, or Draconia as Moss renamed it. The instant we've all flown through the gate, she will start broadcasting the message 'The King Has Returned' so, by the time we get to the castle, everyone should know who we are and expect our arrival."

"I was hoping to announce, 'Behold, the Return of the King,'" Shelley grumped.

"Yes, dear," Bernie soothed, "how dare Fiona get in the way of your nod to *The Return of the King*. We all know it's your favorite movie of the three."

"Did you just call me dear?" Shelley said in awe.

"Oh, brother," Bernie said and I could hear her palming her face again.

This time I laughed until tears ran down my face.

Dawn found me staring at the purple-clad hills a few miles from where we made camp. I remembered seeing pictures of the hills in Scotland covered in purple heather and it looked a lot like what I was seeing right now. I could almost hear the sound of bagpipes playing in the distance. Even though I love my friends and family, it was nice to be able to have this time alone to review what we were going to do today. We were going home.

So far, we had covered thousands of miles but the travel had been relatively uncomplicated. The next part of our journey would end in a battle with Dimitri and his army. I wasn't personally worried that Dimitri could harm me, but my friends and family were vulnerable and could possibly be killed. I was also concerned for those shifters Dimitri had under his influence. I'm sure some of them followed him willingly but imagined that many others did what they had to for the sake of their families.

Dimitri must be stopped, but we would do whatever we could to keep everyone else alive until we could determine if they were loyal to Dimitri or forced to follow him. It made me angry when I imagined the suffering my people had endured under Dimitri's cruelty and that anger burned within me.

"Be careful you don't let your anger turn into hatred, young Alister," a voice said to my right.

Startled I turned to see the lion from my dream. He looked even larger than the last time we met since I was currently standing in my human form. I turned towards him and bowed, "Greetings, An'Ceann, I'm honored."

"Are you sure you don't want to call me Aslan?" He laughed with a deep purr.

"I don't want to offend you, Sir," I countered.

"My son, I wouldn't be offended by that. I've also read those books and Aslan and I have a lot in common, or maybe Aslan has a lot in common with me," I could hear the smile in his voice. "But, that's not why I joined you. I want to give you some perspective." He tossed his head towards the rising sun and somehow I knew he included the hills and flowers in the gesture.

"What do you mean?" I asked.

"This is beautiful, isn't it?" I nodded my response and he continued. "Above ground, the flowers flourish but only because they have healthy nutrients below ground. If we change the soil," he waved his paw and a great swath of flowers wilted, "they can't get what they need and they die. Alister, hatred is poison to your soul. If a person allows hatred to fester, it will eventually take over every part of their life."

"Does that mean I should let Dimitri get away with what he's done?" I snapped but immediately felt ashamed at my response and apologized.

An'Ceann looked at me with kindness and slowly shook his great head. "Not at all. In fact, you are the one who must administer justice to him for everything he has done. Just don't let your anger turn into hatred and then let that hatred take over your life."

"But how will I know if I'm doing that?" I questioned.

"Ask the people who are closest to you, the people you trust, to tell you if you are starting down the wrong path. You can also ask me as well; you call it praying," he said with a grin on his face. "I won't always speak to you as clearly as I'm speaking to you now, but I will answer you in my own way."

He started to turn away from me and then stopped when I took a step towards him. He looked at me and nodded his head at my unspoken request. I threw my arms around him as far as they would go and hugged him tightly. I instantly felt great love, comfort and acceptance from An'Ceann and could hear the rumble in his chest as he spoke to me one last time.

"I'm proud of you Alister. You've accomplished so much already but you still have more to do. Today you will face some challenges you never have before. Remember what I've said, not only will my words help you but you might be able to help someone else with them as well. Until next time," he said and he disappeared, which was a bit awkward as I was still hugging him when he did it and I fell to the springy turf.

"Very funny," I grumbled and heard his fading laughter in my head.

Everyone was packed and ready to go when I returned from my time of solitude. *Let's get this show on the road*, I sent brightly to the group and settled down to get the saddle and harnesses attached to my body. We had done this so many times over the past week, it only took a few minutes before we were all set. Shelley and Bernie climbed on my back and I launched myself into the air. When we reached approximately three hundred feet I began to turn in a wide circle and received some last-minute instructions from Gustav using thought-speak.

Sire, please hover where you are and open a gate to Theria. This will probably be more difficult than any other gate you have created so far because you are in the air. You will have to use more energy to keep it open.

Gustav had explained that the sensation of keeping the gate open would be similar to trying to maintain a hole in a pool as I scooped water. The air would naturally try to close the gate I created.

Allow your memories of Theria to guide you as you open the gate, Gustav continued. *Once it is opened, the rest of us will quickly join you in the air and pass through, then you, Shelley and Bernie will be able to slip through before it closes.*

Sounds good, I sent, *here goes.*

I hovered in the air while planning what I wanted to do. First, I needed to create a gate around fifty feet in diameter. We weren't sure how much room we really needed but I figured that would be enough. Then, I'd open the gate and use my power to keep it open. Once I was ready, I checked with everyone to see how they were doing. After getting positive responses, I got to work. It took more effort to create the gate than I was used to; it felt as if I was trying to run in water up to my knees. I poured more power into my efforts and could feel something starting to happen.

"I can see the air in front of us starting to ripple," Bernie shouted, "I don't know what you're doing but keep doing it."

If I'd been in my human form, sweat would be pouring off me as I strained from the effort to open the gate while keeping us hovering in the air. A sonic boom ripped through the sky where the gate was forming while Shelley and Bernie shouted words of encouragement. If I thought the strain was bad before, now it was almost unbearable. We started to slowly sink back towards the ground so I had to redouble my effort to stay aloft and keep the gate open. Opening my eyes, I could see the dark cerulean blue sky of Theria.

I've got a stable gate, please hurry through. I'm not sure how long I can hold it open, I sent to the group below me.

On our way, Gustav sent.

I dropped the mental connection to focus all my energy on keeping the gate accessible, which was becoming more difficult with each passing second. The weight of the air pushed against the gate like a river pushes against a hastily constructed dam. The more the pressure mounted, the harder it became. The gate was beginning to shrink and I knew it was impossible for me to keep it open on my own. There was no way we were all going to make it through to Theria if I didn't find more energy from somewhere.

I can't hold it, I broadcast, *what do I do?*

Tap into the shifters across the planet of Theria, Mom sent, *use your power as King.*

When I battled with Minos and accepted my role as king, I was connected to thousands of shifters, so I concentrated on what that felt like and opened myself to it again. At once, I could feel hundreds of thousands of tendrils connect to me and infuse me with energy. It became easy to continue hovering in place while keeping the gate open at the same time. There were so many more connections than before, it must be because there was an open gate in front of me. I laughed in delight from the amazing feeling of being connected to so many shifters at once.

Even though I had to keep concentrating on the gate, I was able to explore the connections and where they came from. The longer I was connected the more information I gained. I could actually feel some of the emotions coming from the shifters I was connected to. At first, there was a general feeling of alarm and then one of relief. Instead of pulling energy from the connections, the shifters were willingly pushing power towards me.

We're almost there, hang on Alister, Mom shouted into my head.

I'm actually doing okay now, I sent, *I'm getting more than enough power from the shifters all across Theria.*

Be careful you don't pull too much, Gustav warned, *you could accidentally kill someone if you take all of their energy at once.*

I appreciated the warning but didn't know how to explain to Gustav the sheer amount of power being offered freely to me through the connection. However, things started to change rapidly as Dad passed through the gate into Theria, because just like last time, the power started to flow back out of me towards the shifters who had given it to me to begin with. At first, it was a trickle, but then it changed to a rushing torrent, being siphoned from my body back down the connections we shared. This wouldn't have been too bad if I'd been standing on the ground and not trying to keep the gate open while hovering at the same time. It felt like everything began to move in slow motion as I watched the others follow Dad through the gate. Everything that is, except the flow of power, which sped up.

It was even more of a race now as I watched Gustav fly through with Mom close behind him. All of the extra energy I had gained from the connection was gone and once again I was using only my own power to keep the gate open and didn't have much of that left. Like before, the rest of the tendrils dropped away, except for two that continued to drain energy from my body. I was exhausted and barely able to keep the gate open, and then couldn't do that any longer either.

I panicked as we dropped approximately twenty feet and I could hear Shelley and Bernie yell reflexively as we fell. Looking back up at the gate it seemed to only be about forty feet across as Mom passed through and I was terrified that we would be trapped on this side. Beating my wings, I rushed towards the rapidly shrinking opening, *I have to make it, can't let everyone down, I have to save my people from Dimitri*, I roared and folded my wings and dove through the center of the gate into Theria.

There was another sonic boom behind me a split second after I passed through which marked the closing of the gate. At least that was my assumption but I had to make sure. I watched Dad, Mom and Gustav gliding towards the shore of a lake below our entry point and was relieved that they were safe.

How're you doing? I sent to Bernie and Shelley and swung us around to look where the gate had been.

I think I'm going to be sick, Shelley moaned.

I think I'm going to be sick, again, Bernie muttered. *Sorry about the mess, Alister. I've never liked roller coasters.*

That's okay, I'll take a swim in the lake to get cleaned up.

We hovered in place as I searched for the gate but didn't see anything. Closing my eyes I checked to see if there was a residual opening and discovered the gate was well and truly closed. Pausing for an instant to recover, I realized how exhausted I really was. The peace was broken by a terrifying roar. Opening my eyes and searching for the source of the sound, I saw a flash of green rushing down from my right.

I reacted instinctively and shied away from the flash of sunlight on scales but still felt claws rake across my right wing. There was instant, excruciating pain followed by the sound of a snap as my wing broke. Time slowed as I tracked the movement of the dragon who attacked me and we started to fall from the sky. My right wing was shredded, bloodied and useless for flight. Bernie and Shelley screamed from my back and I could also hear cries of outrage from those who were already on the ground. I tucked my wing close to my side and we began to plummet faster towards the ground. The other dragon must've wheeled around for another attack but because we dropped so suddenly, it passed over our heads with a scream of rage.

I was terrified for Bernie and Shelley; they wouldn't survive if the dragon hit them or let loose with fire. I stretched out my broken wing as far as possible to slow our descent. The pain intensified as the broken bones scraped against each other, but the wing held long enough for me to glide towards the lake. My vision started to fade because of the pain but I couldn't afford to faint or my friends were dead.

I need you to jump into the water as we get closer, I sent, *I need to know you're safe.*

Before they could answer, I heard another roar and chanced a look over my shoulder at the other dragon who had gained on us again. The dragon was ready to release a blast of flame. If it hit them, Bernie and Shelley would be killed. I did the only thing possible and increased my speed of descent towards the water and executed a barrel roll in the air. The flame narrowly missed my friends but hit me squarely instead. The flames scorched my belly and chest and I roared in pain as the flames licked along my scales.

"We're off," Shelley shouted as they dropped into the water. I hoped they were okay but couldn't do anything about it right then. I finished the barrel roll with the intent of fighting off the dragon behind me. Even though it had taken me by surprise, now that I didn't have to worry about my passengers I could defeat it easily because it was much smaller than me.

I pumped my wings, intending to fly up and loop behind the angry dragon and put an end to this fight. As I did so, my right wing, which had begun healing, couldn't handle the strain and snapped again. I bellowed in pain and fell from the sky. My friends and family watched me in horror as I shot past them. I tried to use my left wing to slow my descent but it was too late for that. I careened towards the forest at the edge of the lake. The ground rushed up at me and all I could do was tuck my wings and try to roll when I hit the ground at almost full flight speed.

When I was seven, we took a vacation to California to visit Disneyland and the Pacific Ocean. Dad and I went swimming and he taught me how to body surf. There was one particularly large wave that caught me unawares and I was knocked down and tumbled in the churning water. I ended up tucking myself into a ball to ride out the violence of the surf and even though I was underwater for a bit, I wasn't hurt by the tumbling.

I tried doing the same thing after slamming into the trees on the shoreline but it didn't help. The trees snapped like twigs as I hit them and then bounced off the ground. Even though I tried to keep my wings tucked, I was so weak my limbs were flailing about and I actually cut myself with my own claws and spikes.

Ground...trees...sky...ground...trees...pain...pain...pain, over and over again.

My momentum finally stopped when I slammed into the base of a stone cliff. Everything hurt and I wasn't able to move. I looked down the path of destruction I had created with my body. Giant trees were shattered and lying broken on the ground and there were great gouges in the forest floor where my body struck again, and again and again.

My vision dimmed as I began to fall into unconsciousness. I saw the smaller dragon flying down the path of destruction but couldn't do anything to defend myself. Just before the darkness consumed me, I shouted out in thought-speak. *I failed to Protect the Weak; forgive me.* The last image in my mind before losing consciousness was a bloody dragon's claw reaching for me.

CHAPTER SEVEN

It was dark. The kind that makes you forget you've ever seen light before. Awareness slowly returned to me and I found myself floating on a river of blackness. Moving my arms and legs to test them for injuries, it dawned on me that I was in my human form and feeling weaker than I'd ever felt before. The pain that caused me to lose consciousness had faded to a bad memory and I spent a few minutes wondering if the other dragon had killed me. It must have been a Royal Dragon to cause me so much damage. It figures, the first one I met would try to kill me.

After a minute, or an hour, it became apparent that I was moving faster in the abyss. At first, the speed gradually increased but soon I was careening down the river as fast as if flying at top speed. There wasn't a change in the darkness but I somehow knew I was rushing towards a chasm. My speed increased again as I was catapulted off the edge and began to freefall. I opened my mouth to scream but instead of sound, flames shot from my lips lighting up my environment. There wasn't anything to see but immediately when the flame left my mouth, I transformed into my dragon and let loose a challenging roar. *I am Alister Rex, High King over all of Theria, I will not be stopped.* At once, the darkness was chased away by a blinding white light and I felt strong again.

My senses returned to me in snatches until realization hit me that I was lying on a bed. Opening my eyes, I blinked at the bright light streaming into the room from the open window to the left of my bed. I had never been in this room before but based on the stone blocks, I surmised it was in a castle.

There were tapestries on either side of the window, a red one with a golden drake in the center and the other my standard, red flying dragon on a field of green. To the right of the window there was a great, wooden, chest of drawers and a mirror mounted on the wall. A huge fireplace took most of the wall directly across from the foot of my bed with large overstuffed armchairs in a semi-circle facing it. A magnificent wardrobe, decorated with intricate carvings stood directly across from the chest of drawers that reminded me of the book, *The Lion, the Witch and the Wardrobe* by C.S. Lewis. Next to that was an enormous wooden door that must open to a corridor.

A gentle snore caused me to focus on a girl sitting next to my bed, sleeping with her head on her arms. I couldn't see what she looked like because her long auburn hair was covering her face which was turned away from me. She snored again and blew her hair away from her mouth like a character in a cartoon and I couldn't stop the laugh that rumbled in my chest. My throat was parched so my voice came out as a croak when I tried to speak. "Who are you, and where am I?"

My question startled her awake and she jumped off the chair, which clattered to the floor. Her blue eyes were wide with fright and she trembled as she stared down at me. I was completely vulnerable as I lay on the bed but didn't get a sense of danger from this young woman. My first impression was that she was younger than me, but the more I looked at her, it became apparent she was close to my age. I couldn't help grinning when I noticed she had drool on the left side of her mouth and her hair was sticking up from her head like a bird's nest.

"Hi, I'm Alister," I tried again in an attempt to calm her down. "What's your name?"

"I'm Aileene, and I'm ever so glad you're awake," she replied with a melodious lilt to her voice.

"Me, too," I said encouragingly. "Can you please tell me where I am and if my friends are safe?"

"Oh, I'm so sorry, you've got me so flustered I've forgotten my manners. You are in the castle of Lord Moss, ruler of Draconia. Your friends are guests of his lordship and are resting. The lord's sister, Fiona, was here sitting by your side until I begged her to get some rest and promised to stay until you awoke."

"Thank you, Aileene," I said gratefully. "Do you know what happened to the Royal Dragon who attacked me?"

Aileene blushed, which was exaggerated by her pale complexion. "The dragon who attacked you transformed back into human form when your mother announced who you were, High King," Aileene stammered as she dropped into a curtsey.

"Hmmm, do you happen to know why the dragon attacked me and my friends, to begin with?" I asked suspiciously.

Aileene looked at me with tears brimming in her eyes, threatening to spill over and run down her face. "I'm so sorry," she whispered. "I didn't know who you were and was startled when you appeared out of thin air. I was on patrol like every morning when I felt my energy being drained by a powerful force. I sensed danger but when a drake, a sphinx and a second drake appeared, it was apparent there was nothing to fear from them because they were no match for me. The drain on my power stopped but was instantly followed by an overwhelming feeling of panic and despair. When you appeared, my instincts kicked in because there was an unannounced Royal Dragon in my territory. I had no idea who you were, or why you were here, but I assumed you were an enemy and had to stop you."

"Didn't you see I wasn't fighting back but trying to get away?" I asked with a little heat in my voice.

"I thought it was a trick," she sighed. "You are so much larger than me I figured you were only waiting for your chance to kill me. It wasn't until you rolled and took the blast of my fire on your belly and chest that I realized you were trying to protect the passengers on your back. I was horrified when your wing snapped and you fell to the ground. You were going so fast you must have taken out hundreds of trees as you crashed into them. I finally got the message who you are from Lady Fiona and was flying after you to see if I could help. You were so broken and bloody when I reached you, I was afraid I'd killed you. You passed out just as I landed."

She looked at me so earnestly my heart hurt for her. I could tell she really was sorry for attacking us. I could also sense that she was afraid of what I was going to do to her.

Bernie and Shelley, I sent, *can you please join me? I would like to help Aileene stop feeling guilty about attacking me.*

It's about time you woke up, we were getting bored, Shelley sent but I could sense the relief in his sending.

We'll be right there, Bernie added.

Focusing on Aileene I saw the tears falling freely down her face. "I really am sorry, your Majesty. I don't deserve your leniency, but I beg you to spare the people in this castle," she sobbed.

"Aileene, I wish there'd been a way to let you know we were coming before we surprised you but that wasn't possible. It makes perfect sense why you struck first and I hold you harmless. As for the people in the castle, unless they've done something deserving judgment, I won't hold anyone else accountable for what you did. And as far as I'm concerned, you were just protecting those people who couldn't defend themselves."

She tried to hide the relief on her face as she listened to my words, but I could tell she had been terrified by how I'd react.

"However," I continued, "Sir Arktos and Sir Einhorn need to talk with you and are coming to join us."

The door opened and Bernie walked into the room followed by Shelley. Both of them looked like Knights. They wore armor, had swords on their belts and had on tunics with my royal standard on the front. Aileene turned towards my friends and stood motionless, holding her fisted hands straight by her side. I could scent fear coming from her and hoped Bernie and Shelley could help her feel better. They were staring intently at Aileene when Shelley burst into a grin.

"Hey Alister, I'm glad you finally woke up so you could meet the girl who kicked your butt," Shelley laughed.

"If I hadn't been afraid for my life and terrified that you were going to die, I would have liked to film the beat down to show you whenever you think you're all that," Bernie added.

Aileene whirled towards me with shock on her face. I could tell she was wondering what I would do so I obliged by laughing at my friends.

"I didn't notice you two doing anything to help, nothing except jumping into the water when I told you to," I quipped.

"H...how can you allow them to speak to you that way?" Aileene stammered.

I waved her concern away and slowly got out of bed. Thankfully someone had put some sort of bed clothes on me so I was decent.

"Oh, this is nothing, trust me," I smiled. "We've been friends since we were kids. They actually help me stay grounded and not let my power go to my head."

"We figure we need to get you on our team, Aileene," Shelley chuckled. "We can use words to keep him in line but you're the only one who can really put the smackdown on Alister if he needs it."

Aileene looked stunned and sat heavily on the bed I had just vacated. "I don't understand this at all. I feared the worst after all your companions shouted at me for attacking you. How can you laugh about it as though I did nothing wrong? I attacked and wounded the King."

"Don't forget the bit when he took out half an ancient forest because of your attack, that was my favorite part," Shelley added with a wink at Aileene.

I nodded to Bernie and she approached the bed, sat next to Aileene and held her hand in hers.

"Aileene, there's something you need to understand about King Alister. He has a habit of caring more about the safety of others than he does about his own. If you had killed one of us, he wouldn't be able to forgive so easily but since you only injured him and he seems to be better, he really will let this go and not hold it against you."

"Aileene," I said and got down on one knee so I could easily look at the young woman sitting on the bed. "Why did you attack me?"

She looked confused, "I already told you that I felt the pull of energy and thought we were being attacked by an enemy."

"I know that," I nodded, "but why did you attack me, a much larger dragon who could probably rip you to shreds if I got ahold of you?" I asked.

Aileene thought about the question and the reasons why she put herself in danger. She sat up straighter when she realized the answer to my question. "I thought you were an enemy and I couldn't let you harm the people in this castle. I've never met another Royal Dragon before but do know what we're capable of if we decide to attack. I couldn't let an enemy harm the people under my protection."

I looked into her eyes, saw the earnestness in them and smiled widely at her. Bernie smiled too and I knew that Shelley was reacting the same way to her answer.

"Do you know the motto of the Royal House?" I queried.

Aileene twisted up her face in thought as she searched her memories for the answer but shook her head.

"I don't know if I've been taught that," she sighed. "I've only been tutored on the specifics of Draconia."

"Looks like we'll need to have a discussion with the tutors in the castle," Shelley muttered darkly.

"Yes, we will," I agreed and then turned my attention back to Aileene. "Our motto is *Protect the Weak*, and that is what you were trying to do. To you, I was an enemy and you had to do whatever you could to protect those weaker than yourself. Thank you for that," I said patting her knee as I stood.

Bernie put her arm around the stunned young woman and hugged her.

"Uh, oh," Shelley said, "looks like Bernie has adopted you into our group. I just hope I'm not too much of a bad influence on you."

Aileene laughed and looked hopeful.

"I think we should go find the others. I'm hungry after all the healing I had to do and I'd like to find out what's been going on."

"Your mom has been talking with her brother," Shelley replied.

"How has that been so far?" I asked.

"Loud," Bernie answered with a snicker.

I started for the door but stopped when Shelley cleared his throat behind me and stifled a laugh as he said, "Sire, while I am sure everyone will be most grateful that you are back on your feet again. I'm not sure they'll want you to appear in your royal pajamas."

I looked down at myself and saw the nightshirt. "I suppose you're right. I don't think it would project the same sense of authority if my royal knees were on display."

Bernie and Aileene giggled behind me and the sound of Aileene's laughter filled me with a sense of joy, contentment and a warmth in my chest I'd never felt before.

After a light meal and a quick bath, I felt more like myself again. Shelley stayed with me to fill me in on everything that had happened since I lost consciousness in the forest. He told me he was suitably impressed with the amount of destruction I caused while tumbling through the forest. Apparently our companions reached my side moments after I lost consciousness and they saw my charred chest, shredded wing, broken, bloody body and a female Royal Dragon standing over my still form. Mom gave vent to her fury and told Aileene who I was and exactly what she would do to her if she harmed me again. Even though plowing through the trees and ground hadn't added to my injuries, I had done a good job of carving myself up with my own spikes and claws as I tumbled along the ground.

Lord Moss and his entourage arrived then and Aileene transformed into human so she could explain what happened to everyone at the same time. Lord Moss and Mom were shouting at each other, our companions and Lord Moss' people were starting to face off against each other and all the while Aileene was standing next to me.

Things might have gone from bad to worse when Mom attempted to attack her brother after he came close to my unconscious body, but Aileene intervened. She growled loudly enough that everyone stopped talking and decided not to face the angry dragon currently in the form of a young woman. Aileene leaned down, whispered something in my ear and I transformed from my dragon into my human form. She gently gathered me in her arms, her tears falling on my face, manifested her wings and flew with me back to the castle. The others followed closely behind her because that was their only option.

Mom and Dad chased everyone out of my room while they washed and tended my wounds and put me to bed. The Einhorns attempted to use some of the natural healing magic they possess as unicorns to heal me but it's difficult for someone who isn't a Royal Dragon to either harm or heal one of us. Everyone took turns sitting by my side for the two days I was in a healing sleep. Aileene finally shooed them all out and took over the watch, about an hour before I awoke.

"Dude," Shelley said before we left the room to join Bernie and Aileene, "thank you for saving us. If we would've been hit by the dragon fire, we'd be goners."

Giving Shelley a bro hug, I answered him, my voice thick with emotion. "I don't know what I'd do without you and Bernie."

"I don't know," Shelley answered with a twinkle in his eye, "I'm sure you've noticed how cute Aileene is, and she's a Royal Dragon. Maybe you won't need me and Bernie as much in the future." He grinned and waggled his eyebrows.

Laughing as I punched him in the arm, I answered, "Oh, I noticed, but you're a dork. Let's meet up with the girls."

When we left the room, Bernie and Aileene were waiting for us in the hallway. By the grin on Bernie's face and the blush that crept up Aileene's neck and face, I figured they heard our conversation.

You knew they were in the hallway, didn't you? I sent to Shelley.

Yep! And you would have too if you weren't so busy thinking about how cute Aileene is. Laughter came through his thoughts.

"What's the plan?" I asked clearing my throat.

"Everyone was going to meet in the throne room, once you were ready," Bernie replied. "I sent a message that we're on our way."

She turned and led the way and Shelley brought up the rear. Aileene and I walked side-by-side down the long hallway. The floor and walls were made of square-cut stone blocks and the halls were lit by lights on the walls and in chandeliers hanging from the ceiling. They looked similar to electric lights on Earth. We walked on brightly colored, woven rugs and I was impressed by the attention to detail on the tapestries that lined the walls.

"Aileene, do you live in the castle?" I asked nervously. Since Shelley made the comment about how cute she was, I felt a bit more awkward around her now.

"Yes," she answered.

After a few seconds, she must have decided to put me out of my misery and whispered, "And, I think you're pretty cute, too."

I don't remember the rest of the walk but must have had a goofy look on my face as we entered the throne room because Mom stopped arguing with the person sitting on the throne and gave me a quizzical look.

I'll explain later, I sent. *What's going on?*

I'm just arguing with my idiot brother, Mom huffed.

Bernie stopped a few feet into the room and loudly announced, "His Royal Highness, Alister Rex, High King of all Theria, Opener of Gates, Righter of Wrongs, Avenger of Blood and Servant of An'Ceann."

Wow, Bernie can even make you sound impressive, Shelley sent. He must have broadcast it to me and Aileene since I heard her gently cough to cover a giggle.

This isn't the time, but I'll get you for that, I threatened.

Looking forward to it, Stretch, Shelley countered.

I walked towards the raised dais at the front of the room and Bernie took a position on my left while Shelley stood to the right of Aileene, who was walking next to me. The four of us walked towards our families and the man seated on the throne. He had a narrow face and piercing dark-brown eyes that were almost black. His black hair was shoulder length and I imagined the look of superiority was permanently etched on his face. His eyes hardened when he saw Aileene walking next to me. His voice was rich and cultured when he greeted me as I stopped and stood before his throne.

"Welcome to Draconia, King Alister, I hope that your shame at being bested by young Aileene here will not cause you to punish her too harshly for injuring you," he said, his words dripping with disdain.

"Why you pompous..." Mom began but I held up my hand to stop her.

I didn't say anything while studying Moss. He tried to project an attitude of indifference but I could smell his fear and see his knuckles were white as he gripped the throne. Sweat also began to bead on his brow so I knew he wasn't as relaxed as he wanted me to think.

"Please tell me, Lord Moss, why would I seek to punish someone for upholding the laws of our kingdom?"

"Because she attacked you," he spat.

"She attacked because she thought I was an enemy and was seeking to protect you and the others in this castle. I have already told her this but will declare it to you as well. Aileene has earned my respect and I honor her willingness to *Protect the Weak*."

I turned and bowed to a shocked Aileene and she curtsied in return.

Turning back to Moss, I continued, my voice firm. "However, I am concerned that she did not know this was something important to the High King."

Moss squirmed uncomfortably on his throne and I watched a range of emotions cross his face. His first response was shock, then guilt, followed by fear and finally settling on the angry visage he had when we first entered the room.

There was a genuine concern in my voice as I continued speaking to Moss. "Please tell me, why are you so angry? I've never done anything to harm you in any way."

He pointed to my mom. "Do you think I don't know why you brought her here? You seek to depose me and place her on the throne instead. Where have you been High King? For thirteen years the Kingdom of Theria has been silent and suddenly my sister appears, unannounced, claiming to need my help. She has been banished from this kingdom; I have every right to have her executed for violating my decree," he raged, spittle flying from his mouth.

The throne room became deathly quiet as I continued to stare at Moss as he attempted to shrink back into his throne. "Let me make this clear to you," I said with steel in my voice. "Albert and Fiona Drake are my parents. They were asked by King Phillip and Queen Beatrice, my royal parents, to take me in and raise me as their own if something ever happened to them. When they were betrayed and killed by their friend Dimitri, these two put their lives on hold to raise me. They taught me how to serve others, they taught me the ways of An'Ceann and how to *Protect the Weak*. They are here with me now, because I am in great need and this was the closest kingdom we could enter without opening a gate straight into the High Kingdom where Dimitri is waiting to attack innocents. We are here to prevent the loss of lives."

Moss paled as I continued to look at him. I could feel my eyes blazing and felt my body begin to swell in anger. "It wasn't my intent to remove you from your throne but now I wonder. You are so full of bitterness towards your sister, hatred is radiating from you like a furnace. You wronged your sister when she married Albert Drake. You were in the wrong when you banished her instead of being content that you got to rule, which is what you wanted. You let your fear, that your sister would come and take back what is rightfully hers, consume you and that fear has turned to hate."

I looked over to my mom, who was tightly holding my dad's hand. There were tears in her eyes.

"It is within my right, as High King, to rip the throne from you and banish you from your own kingdom. That would be a fitting punishment for the way you treated my mom and dad in the past and the way you continue to treat them today. Do you deny that this is within my power?" I stopped talking but continued to stare at the man as he considered my words. His shoulders slumped and he bowed his head in resignation at my judgment.

"No, Sire," he mumbled. "I cannot deny that you are within your rights to do such a thing."

I nodded my head and looked between Moss and my mom. He continued to stare at his lap so he didn't see Mom minutely shaking her head. I breathed a sigh of relief and then started talking again.

"Look at me Lord Moss, Ruler of Eutheria."

He looked at me, defeat evident in his body language.

"I said it is within my right to do these things, not that I will do these things. Based on the connection you have to me, it is clear that you are loyal to the High King. I do not sense oppression among the shifters in this kingdom through the same connection, so you must be a benevolent ruler. However, you have been unjust to Albert and Fiona Drake and that injustice cannot continue. Fritz Einhorn, attend to me and record this royal decree."

"At once, Sire," Fritz called and then sent a runner from the room to bring him writing utensils and paper. There was complete silence while we waited for the items he had requested. Fritz sat at a nearby desk and arranged what he needed once the runner returned and handed them to Fritz. He nodded to me so I turned back to address Moss.

"As of now, the unjust law that the ruler of this kingdom can only marry a natural-born drake is null and void. Every instance of this law having ever been applied will be blotted from the records as well. Am I clear?"

Moss nodded and continued to look at me. Surprisingly, there was a glimmer of hope in his eye.

"Secondly, unless there is a reason I'm unaware of, this kingdom will once again be called Eutheria. I think we've had quite enough of Draconia, don't you?"

Moss nodded.

I continued. "The banishment of Albert and Fiona Drake is rescinded and will be completely stricken from the records as well." Moss nodded again. "And finally, and this is the most difficult thing of all, James Moss and Fiona Drake you are hereby ordered by your King, to immediately leave my presence and work out your issues with each other. I was recently reminded that hatred is a poison to our souls and if left to fester it will take over every part of our lives. You two have allowed your anger to turn to hatred for each other and that has affected you in more ways than you can imagine. This cannot continue."

I looked at Mom after issuing my decrees and she nodded her head in agreement. Dad hugged her tightly and she put her head on his chest and began to cry. I looked at Moss expectantly and he rose from his seat.

"Sire, you have been more gracious to me than I deserve, thank you." He walked over to where Dad and Mom were standing. "Albert, I am sorry that I have caused you so much pain. Come, Fifi, let's go to the alcove where we used to hide when we were children so we can do as our King commands." He held out his hand and after a slight hesitation, she put her hand in his and he led her away.

"Well, if there isn't anything else to discuss," I began, "let's find some food, I'm starving."

We ate our meal in the banquet hall and it was delicious. After so long on Middle Earth it was a treat to sit inside at a table while enjoying good food. Shelley entertained everyone with stories from our journey and we didn't really mind that he embellished a bit as he shared. As we laughed together tensions from the Eutherian shifters melted away and they eventually joined in by telling amusing stories of their own. I could tell the residents and servants of the castle weren't used the relaxed atmosphere we brought with us and kept darting nervous glances my way when Shelley said something humorous at my expense.

Fritz Einhorn used thought-speak to guide me in matters of protocol so I didn't make a fool of myself during the meal. Unfortunately, as High King, I was required to sit at the head of the table rather than next to my friends or Aileene where I'd rather be. While eating I caught Aileene staring at me as often as she caught me staring at her. I really wanted to spend time talking with her about her experiences as a Royal Dragon.

A regal woman sitting to my right leaned in close to me and whispered, "how did you know?"

"Pardon me, Lady—?" I queried.

"Please forgive me, your Majesty, I am Lady Bronwyn," she

blushed. "How did you know that Lord Moss and I are true mates, but are unable to do anything about it because I am a manticore?"

Stunned, I thought about her question and its implications to the situation in Eutheria. Finally, I answered her honestly. "I didn't know any of that when I made my decree. I'm happy that you and Lord Moss will be able to finally realize happiness but why didn't he invalidate the law on his own?"

Lady Bronwyn looked down at her plate as she answered. "There are a few reasons, the first being, he used the law to take the throne from Lady Fiona when she married Lord Albert and then banished them. Second, he thought he didn't have the authority to invalidate a law your own royal father, King Phillip, let stand. Since there hasn't been any word from the High King for over thirteen years, and we only met about ten years ago, he didn't feel he could make that decision on his own." Lady Bronwyn looked at me fiercely, "Lord Moss is absolutely loyal to the throne of the High King."

I nodded my agreement and motioned for her to continue.

"But the most important reason was his fear of what Lady Fiona would do if she ever found out about us. He let that fear dictate his actions. He is a good ruler, a good shifter and a good man, he really isn't the angry person you saw today. Thank you for showing leniency and for forcing him to work things out with his sister." She reached out her hand as if to touch me and folded her hands back in front of her. I reached out and placed my hand on top of hers.

"I'll let you in on a little secret," I smiled. "I may not have known what was going on behind the scenes but I feel certain An'Ceann gave me a bit of a nudge to help resolve this problem. I was recently reminded about the destructive power of hate and that definitely influenced my decision." She sat back in her chair, absolutely stunned by my words. As I finished my meal, I noticed Aileene smiling at me when I chanced another glance her way.

We reconvened in the throne room after the midday meal and Fritz directed me to the throne. Fritz and Frieda continued to whisper suggestions in my mind as I dealt with issues Lord Moss was unable to handle. After Shelley escorted the last petitioner out the door I was able to get down to the business of freeing the Kingdom of Theria from Dimitri's oppression.

I called General Arktos and General McIntyre, the commander of the Eutherian army, to stand before me.

"Generals, please put together a battle plan so we can conquer Dimitri's troops with the least amount of fatalities in the shortest amount of time," they nodded to me and as they left the room; Miriam joined them.

After they left the room, Dad came and stood before me. He was wearing the livery of my court but had added a touch of his own. I'm not sure where he got them but he was wearing a pair of green sweatpants with flying red dragons printed all over them. He smirked as he noticed my eyes widen at his ridiculous choice of pants.

"Hey Dad, how're you doing?"

He got serious as he looked around the room. "I never thought I would ever stand here again and it feels a bit strange. Son, I know your mom puts up a bold front but her heart was broken all those years ago by what Moss did to her. I got your mom, which is all I wanted, but she lost her baby brother. Thanks for forcing them to work this out. They haven't spoken since the day of our wedding and I know she has ached about it since then. You did a good thing, I'm proud of you."

It probably wasn't proper protocol, but I leaped from the throne and threw my arms around my dad.

"Thank you," I whispered as I hugged him tightly, "that means a lot. I took a wild guess that it was the right thing to do."

Dad hugged me tighter and whispered back, "No one could tell, you're doing great." We stood there for a minute and I basked in the warmth of his embrace and praise.

Finally, I let go and stepped back. Dad put his hands on my upper arms and squeezed gently as he looked intently at my face.

"Just remember," he said, "you don't have to do all this alone. It's a lot of weight to carry at your age. We're here to guide you and keep you from making the same mistakes we did when we were your age. The stories I could tell you about the dumb things Phillip, Stavros and I would get into," he smiled as he remembered some of them.

I looked over at Fritz. "What about him, didn't he do dumb things?"

Dad looked over at his old friend and said with great fondness. "Him? No, I think Fritz was born an old man, he never got into trouble."

Fritz's snort sounded so much like a unicorn I had to double-check he hadn't shifted. "Where would you miscreants be if I hadn't been there to talk some reason into your insanity?" Frieda rolled her eyes while the rest of us laughed good-naturedly.

Giving Dad another quick hug I retook my seat on the throne while he went to talk with Fritz and Frieda.

Aileene stood in front of me, hands fisted at her sides, and bowed stiffly. I smiled at her and inclined my head for her to speak.

"Your Majesty, I would like to be part of the battle, and would like your permission to fly by your side," Aileene requested formally.

I thought over the benefits of having her join us. Who was I kidding? I'd just love to be able to spend more time with her but had to ask why she wanted to do this. "Don't you think it would be better for you to stay here to make sure this kingdom is safe?" I asked.

Alister, she sent, *it's important that I come with you. Our first meeting was less than ideal, and that was my fault, but I'm going to need you to trust me.*

I thought about what she said, but also what she wasn't saying, *You've had a vision of An'Ceann, haven't you?*

She looked shocked but answered me anyway, *I wasn't sure if I could tell you about it, but yes I did. An'Ceann came to me while I was in your room waiting for you to recover. He told me about our ancient history and how I would need to make a choice to follow his ways or keep doing things the way I had been doing them. He told me that this is the same choice he gives to every Royal Dragon at a certain point.*

That's the same thing he told me, I sent, *and I chose to follow him.*

The look of joy on Aileene's face melted my heart. *I was hoping you had, based on your decisions that you've made since being here, but I was still a little worried. I've made the same choice too!* Aileene gushed.

Smiling brightly, I spoke aloud. "Aileene of Eutheria, I am honored by your request to fly by my side as we battle the enemies of Theria and gratefully accept."

There was enthusiastic cheering from those who were still in the throne room but I only had eyes for the beauty standing before me.

"Dimitri doesn't know what's coming for him," Bernie muttered beside me, "I hope I get to see the look on his face when he sees both of you flying towards him."

"I'll make sure to take a good mind shot to share with you; this is going to be something we'll watch for years to come," Aileene answered Bernie but she looked at me with a gleam in her eye. I couldn't help chuckling at what I saw there.

CHAPTER EIGHT

Shelley, Bernie and I were in the throne room tossing a ball around when Mom and Moss came out of the alcove after dinner. They were walking arm in arm and were actually laughing together. At first, they didn't notice we were there, but when Moss saw me, he instantly stood straighter and put his arrogant mask in place. Mom took one look at him, started laughing and slapped him on the chest with her hand.

"Hey doofus, you don't have to do that in front of Alister, just be yourself," she said in an exasperated tone.

"Hi, Mom, it seems like you're doing better," I smiled and walked over to give her a hug.

"Thank you for the gentle butt-kicking son. It's just what I needed to finally let this go," Mom said as she squeezed me back. "Son, let me officially introduce you to my baby brother, your Uncle James."

Moss looked aghast as I turned to look at him, and I couldn't help laughing when his mouth dropped open but nothing came out. Deciding to tweak him a little more I went in for a bear hug and lifted him off the floor.

"Hi, Uncle James, it's so much nicer to meet you this way," I said and set him down where he stumbled until he regained his balance.

"Unc...Uncle James," he stammered, "you'd accept me as family, after all I've done?"

I shrugged my shoulders. "Sure, if you and Mom are good and she's forgiven you, then we're good. Although I suggest you make things right with Dad, too. He's been a bit perturbed with you for treating his wife the way you did."

Moss looked abashed and hung his head. "I've got a lot to apologize for." He looked back up at me and whispered, "I don't deserve this, how could you forgive me?"

"I recently learned that I can choose to forgive or I can choose to hold onto my anger which will lead to hate, which will in turn poison my soul. To be honest, there's too much to do to hold grudges that aren't mine. If Mom can choose to forgive you, I can too. Mom and Dad raised me on the teachings of An'Ceann and I would much rather live this way than the alternative."

Mom wiped a tear from her eye. "Thank you son, I chose not to forgive my brother, and it really was a poison in my life; I feel better than I have for centuries. How did you get to be so mature?" she asked.

I shrugged my shoulders and smiled, "I don't know, must get it from Dad." We laughed together and they excused themselves to go find my dad.

"Did you know Dad managed to bring his sweatpants?" I asked Mom as she was leaving.

"Of course," she said over her shoulder and winked at me, "who do you think packed them? Bernie and Shelley aren't the only ones who need to help keep you grounded. It's part of a parent's job to embarrass their children." My two Knights snickered.

"Don't you two start," I ground out after Mom and Moss left the room.

Bernie snorted, "I'm not sure I know what you mean, what could we possibly tease you about?"

"Yes, we would never bring up your dad's fashion choices or how he'll influence others in your new court. Although, I must admit your new standard did look rather unique plastered all over a pair of sweats," Shelley chortled.

"Oh brother," I moaned.

It wasn't until after breakfast the next day that Generals Arktos and McIntyre were ready with a battle strategy. My original traveling companions, along with Aileene, Uncle James, Lady Bronwyn and I met in the war room which was located near the roof of the castle. There was a wide doorway with a secure portcullis which could be raised or lowered as needed. I assumed this opening would allow messengers to fly in and out so they could give updates and receive instructions. There was also a large round table in the middle of the room, where a map of the entire planet of Theria was laid out. We were gathered around that table.

Even though the castle looked medieval in design, the map was high tech and interactive. We could zoom in to any portion of the map when we needed to highlight what we were looking for. General McIntyre touched the area corresponding to the Kingdom of Theria and used his thumb and forefinger to zoom in.

"Based on the intelligence provided by you, Dimitri is most likely here with his army." We could see the large meadow where we calculated Dimitri had gathered. "We don't really have any idea of the number or types of troops he has, but it would be safe to assume he has an army of powerful shifters."

"Since the King has instructed us to create a battle plan with the least amount of lives lost," General Arktos continued, "we will need a way to neutralize as many enemy combatants as promptly as possible in a non-lethal way."

"We're assuming a portion of Dimitri's army is being coerced to fight for him, based on what Wu has told us about his own experiences," General McIntyre added, "but we have no way of knowing who they are or how many of these will be on the field of battle."

We stood looking at the map and pondered the problem. Bernie spoke up, "When we were on Middle Earth, King Alister was able to force an enemy to shift from his minotaur to human form. Could he do this on a large scale?"

"Middle Earth?" General McIntyre asked.

"It's a long story, I'll explain later," General Arktos muttered while Shelley snickered.

"It's possible, but it would take a tremendous amount of energy," Gustav added.

"More energy than it took for him to hold open the gate?" Miriam asked.

"Hmmm..." Gustav began and looked like he was doing calculations in his head. "It would depend on how large the army is and how quickly the rest of us could subdue the shifters in their human forms."

"Let's assume I can amass enough power to shift every soldier at the same time. How long will it take us to train our troops to subdue them without killing?" I asked.

"I would say, three days of training and we should be ready," General McIntyre answered and General Arktos nodded.

"Okay," I agreed, "let's go with this plan. Next question, how long will it take us to get our army to Theria?"

"Does anyone else find it confusing that the planet is named Theria, and the High King's seat of power is also called Theria? Maybe we should rename it something like Narnia?"

"No," I answered.

"Lothlorien?" Shelley tried again.

"No," I repeated.

"Gotham City?" He asked.

"Absolutely not!" I cried.

"Mount Olympus?" He said as he looked at me and raised one eyebrow.

I pretended to think about that one for a few seconds and then shook my head, "Nope, I think we'll just leave it Theria."

"Fine, just trying to add something to the discussion," he grumped and crossed his arms over his massive chest.

"There, there," Bernie said as she patted his shoulder, "you can't rename every planet, country, and town you want. We have to draw the line somewhere."

Everyone in the room laughed when Shelley stuck his tongue out at Bernie and she grabbed it before he could put it back in his mouth.

"Outh, thad hurth," he mumbled.

Lord Moss laughed as he looked at me. "I like the way your team works."

"Yeah, we put the fun in dysfunctional," I grinned. "Okay, break time's over, let's finish planning this."

General McIntyre looked confused so I took pity on him and prompted, "You were about to tell me how long it will take us to get our army to Theria."

"Oh, yes," he nodded, "well, Sire, we may have a problem with that. We are unable to get into the Kingdom of Theria because of the protective shield surrounding it."

“We think that King Alister will be able to remove the shield with some of his blood,” Gustav added.

“In that case, Sire, if you can create a gate from this location," he pointed to the training field outside of this castle, "to here," he pointed to another large field approximately five miles from the one where we assumed Dimitri was located, "we should be able to move rather rapidly once the shield has been dealt with."

That took me by surprise. "I didn't know it was possible to create gates from one place to another on the same planet. That would have been easier than flying thousands of miles across Middle Earth."

Dad joined the discussion at that point. "This only works if you are familiar with the place you are trying to gate to. Since none of us had been to those locations on Middle Earth it wouldn't have worked. However, all of us from Theria, including you three, are familiar with all the locations around the palace. We used to hold a festival in this location every year. You kids loved to go there when you were younger."

"I remember that place," I exclaimed, "they had the best cotton candy—wait, was that something else shifters introduced to Earth?"

Gustav shook his head. "Believe it or not some things seem to be universal to every dimension, cotton candy is one of them."

Nodding, I continued. "So, I'll open the gate to the fairgrounds, we'll march our army swiftly to meet Dimitri in battle and I'll force the enemy shifters to change. Once they've changed to their human forms, our soldiers will subdue them. Do I understand the plan correctly?"

"Yes," General Arktos answered, "the plan is fairly simple, it just won't be easy."

"Aren't we forgetting about someone?" Aileene asked and I looked at her with a puzzled expression. "What about Dimitri?"

"I was assuming I would be able to force him to change as well," I answered.

"That will be difficult if he still has one of these," Frieda said as she pulled her thought medallion out from the front of her dress, "since Dimitri used to be part of the Inner Circle, he was given a medallion. This offers a form of protection the other shifters won't have."

"I'll take care of distracting Dimitri until King Alister is able to join me," Aileene spoke up.

"That might not be the best idea, my dear," Lord Moss answered, "it is possible that Dimitri was able to create weapons from the bodies of the former King and Queen. If he has weapons made from the remains of Royal Dragons, you could be injured or killed."

The room sobered as we considered this possibility. I was still hopeful that my parents were alive but had to seriously consider what Moss suggested.

"I don't care," Aileene said defiantly. "I'm the only one who can do this. The rest of you are needed to keep the soldiers alive, King Alister's power is needed to keep the shifters in their human forms and I'm nearly indestructible."

"Unless you are wounded by a weapon made from the bones or scales of my parents," I added sadly.

I can't ask you to risk yourself that way. You are too precious. If something happens to me, it will be up to you to keep all of Theria safe, I sent to her.

Aileene turned towards me and her eyes blazed with anger. "You aren't asking me, I'm telling you that I'm going to help and you can either work me into your battle plans, or you will have to fight me to stop me. I will do this for you, for all of us." Aileene was breathing hard as if she had just finished a race and was searching my face to see if I accepted what she just told me.

Please, she added in my mind.

Looking into her fierce eyes I knew I wanted her by my side in this battle, and beyond that as well.

"Very well, my Lady, but if you're going to fight, you will need more training than you already have. Gustav will work with you in your human form, and I will work with you in your dragon form—it won't be pleasant," I cautioned.

Aileene lifted her chin and replied, "I'm ready. I've already kicked your butt once; I look forward to doing it again."

Shelley and Bernie laughed. "She's got you there Stretch, just try not to destroy any more forests this time," Shelley added.

The next three days would be grueling, but I knew we needed every hour of them to be ready to face Dimitri. The first morning I was awake before sunrise and was filled with an even greater sense of urgency than I had experienced before. The night before, I had the same repeating dream but with a huge difference. This time, neither of my parents spoke to me and their dragons were looking haggard and unhealthy. If I were to find my parents alive, we would have to defeat Dimitri at once so we could begin the search for them. Even though I was chafing at the necessary three day delay I knew we couldn't rush our training if we wanted to limit casualties.

While Aileene worked with Gustav, I practiced with our troops. The plan was to force half of them to shift to their human forms while the other half subdued those who were forced to shift. The first time I tried was a disaster. I'd gotten so used to my friends and me wearing thought medallions that I forgot that when other shifters transformed back into humans, they were naked. It was so surprising for me to see a field full of naked humans, I was unable to keep them in their human forms for longer than a few seconds. The ones I forced to change shifted back before they could be captured.

Gathering more power for the second attempt I managed to force them to hold their human forms longer, but forced everyone to shift at the same time. Our side had started in their human forms and were forced to shift into their natural forms while those who started in their shifter forms were forced into their human forms. If we were looking for a way to destroy the enemy, we would have succeeded but we weren't any closer to a deathless alternative.

We took a break while I contemplated the problem. Opening the connection I shared with shifters, I was able to sense each one on our practice field. When I closed my eyes, I could also see the connections moving between myself and the troops around me. As I pushed my awareness further, I could sense a blazing presence nearby that could only be Aileene. As I studied these tendrils of power, I was able to broadcast a feeling of hope and victory. The life force of each shifter grew a little brighter and I could sense Aileene's amusement through the connection we shared. Muting the connection with Aileene, I concentrated on the others who surrounded me. Even though I wasn't consciously pulling power, I could feel my energy reserves filling up with gifts from each shifter nearby.

Slipping into a meditative state, by breathing in through my mouth and out through my nose, I sent the connective tendrils farther out so they could cover all the shifters in the Kingdom of Eutheria. By sending that same feeling of hope through all the connections there was a large draw on my energy. But, once the sense of hope was received there was a tidal wave of power which came back to me; much greater than what I sent out. My internal reservoir expanded to hold the increased energy.

Opening my eyes, I announced that we should try again and the mock battle was reset. Transforming and launching myself into the sky, I connected myself to those shifters who had been designated as enemy troops. Once they transformed into their shifter forms, I signaled our attack with a roar and sent the change command through the established connections. Immediately, those troops transformed back to human which was unfortunate for those who had been flying. Thankfully they hadn't been that high and would heal rapidly. Using their own energy against them, I was able to keep those playing the part of the enemy transformed, while my side subdued them. Even after releasing the connection, I still had a lot of power remaining.

Everyone cheered at our success, even those who were still bound. If we were quick enough, and had overwhelming numbers, we could achieve victory with relatively few casualties. Of course, much of this would depend on how many shifters were following Dimitri of their own free will. Those we would have to subdue the old-fashioned way, superior strength. Rather than dwell on the negatives, I transformed and joined my team in celebration. It had been a good training session.

I asked for a private meeting with Gustav and Uncle James in the castle over our midday meal. After our food was served and we were alone, I broached the topic that concerned me.

"Thank you for meeting with me on such short notice," I began.

"You have but to ask, Sire," Moss started but I held up my hand to stop him.

"Sorry, but since it's just the three of us, can you just call me Alister? When we're not in a formal setting, I'll call you Uncle James or Moss, whichever you prefer."

"Moss will be fine, Alister," he hesitated over my name and smiled nervously.

"Get used to it. Phillip was the same way when he was amongst friends and family," Gustav added.

"Okay, now that we have that out of the way, I'm concerned about the battle with Dimitri. What if he has a Royal Dragon of his own he can bring out against us?"

Moss and Gustav exchanged a glance and I knew they had information that hadn't been shared with me yet. As I watched them have a silent conversation I found it amusing to see the different expressions flit across their faces. They finally ended up glaring at each other but Moss relented.

"Fine," he breathed, "but if Alister roasts me alive, it's your fault."

"That doesn't sound ominous, or anything," I muttered and gave my full attention to Moss.

He held up his hands in a warding gesture. "It's really not that bad, if you think about it. In fact, you might actually be happy, well, maybe not happy, but not really upset by this news, I hope."

Gustav laughed and decided to take pity on Moss. "Alister, Dimitri won't have a Royal Dragon because Aileene is the only other Royal Dragon alive right now."

"How is that possible?" I asked.

Gustav sighed heavily. "This would have been something your parents eventually would have taught you, but since they're not here, this falls to me."

"We could get Fiona to tell him," Moss said hopefully.

Gustav paused to think that over so I interrupted him. "Nope, you two are here so you get to tell me. I'll do my best not to roast anyone," I smiled wickedly.

Moss gulped and began. "During the dark times, there were Royal Dragons ruling each of the shifter kingdoms. The wars were terrible as these dragons fought for territories and mates. The females were just as ferocious as the males and the loss of life was unimaginable. Finally, there were only two Royal Dragons left."

"Dóchas and Síocháin," I said.

"Correct," Moss continued, "however their unborn daughter, Athas, was still in her egg, so that would have been the third Royal Dragon, as far as anyone knew."

"Wait," I held up my hand, "if there were only the three of them, where did Athas' mate come from?"

Gustav continued the story. "During the dark times there were clutches of Royal Dragon eggs hidden on every continent. A dragon hatches from one of these every time an heir hatches from the egg laid by the current Queen. If the heir is male, a female is hatched elsewhere and vice versa. This is a closely guarded secret only known to the rulers of each kingdom and the High King's closest advisors."

"So, does Dimitri know this?" I asked.

Gustav shook his head. "No, Fiona and I are the only members of our Inner Circle to have this knowledge. Fiona because she was heir to the throne of Eutheria and me because it is one of the duties of my role as Historian to convey this knowledge as needed."

I held my silence for a short time as I digested what Gustav had revealed. "Wait," I held up my hand, "so that means that Aileene hatched the same day as me?" Moss and Gustav nodded and I continued. "But she was hatched in Eutheria and we're the only two Royal Dragons alive on the entire planet?" I didn't mention that my parents could still be alive, I didn't want to go down that rabbit hole again.

"I know this is another difficult thing that you have to face, Alister," Gustav said kindly, "but for some reason, this is how An'Ceann has arranged things."

"I'll have to bring this up the next time we have a conversation," I muttered and would swear there was an echo of laughter in my head. Waving off the curious looks from Moss and Gustav I said, "Never mind. So, if I understand you correctly, Aileene and I were literally made for each other, and are fated to become a mated pair?"

Moss looked abashed. "This isn't fair, but it is the way things have been since your ancestors brought peace by uniting the kingdoms. If things had been different, and you hadn't had to flee Theria, you and Aileene would have known each other from childhood and would have been married as true mates before you took the throne."

"I'm not ready to get married," I complained, "although I would like to get to know Aileene much better than I already do."

"I know she is looking forward to training with you this afternoon. This will be the first time either of you has trained with another Royal Dragon. You will need to proceed with caution; you could severely injure yourselves if you aren't careful," Gustav warned.

"I'll do my best," I replied, "since you trained with her this morning, what can you tell me about her fighting style?"

Gustav chuckled. "I don't think I want to share her strategies with you. But, you shouldn't underestimate her. I will be interested in what you find out."

“There's something else I would like to ask about Aileene.” After receiving nods of acceptance from Moss and Gustav I continued. “When we talked about the motto of the Royal House, she didn't have any idea it was *Protect the Weak.* Can you please explain why that is?”

Moss hung his head in shame. “King Phillip and Queen Beatrice knew Aileene had hatched in Eutheria but commanded me to keep it a secret until the time when she would join your family in Theria. When she was hatched, I decided to start calling the kingdom Draconia as a way to assert my authority and if I'm honest, it was a way for me to take a dig at my sister. Even though Fiona and I weren't speaking to each other, the King still supported me as ruler of Eutheria. Your mother, the Queen, always encouraged Fiona to make peace with me but both of us were too stubborn. When all communication stopped coming from Theria and we were unable to break through the magical barrier to find out what happened, I feared the worst.”

“And what was that?” I asked.

“I'm ashamed to admit it but I feared Fiona had somehow convinced the King and Queen to take Aileene from my care by force and replace me on the throne with Fiona.”

“That doesn't make sense,” I said in confusion. “An'Ceann had entrusted Aileene into your care and I'm certain they would've assured you of this.”

Moss nodded his head. “It's true, they did, but you were also correct when you said I let fear overwhelm me and that fear turned to hatred for my sister. The longer the silence continued, the more concerned I became and Draconia, I mean Eutheria, became more isolated. Even though we taught Aileene the way of An'Ceann, I never used the phrase, *Protect the Weak.* I am ashamed of the way I behaved during the years of silence. I once again ask your forgiveness.”

From everything I’d seen so far, Moss was a good ruler for Eutheria. His people were happy and they were following the ways of An'Ceann and the High King whether they knew it or not. It must have been extremely difficult for the rest of the shifter kingdoms to move forward while not knowing what had happened in Theria. With those things at the forefront of my mind, I answered Moss.

“It seems to me that even though you were consumed with hatred for your sister, you still were able to rule with honor, integrity and lead your people well. Thank you for your faithfulness to the teachings of An'Ceann as well as the laws of the Kingdom of Theria. Your loyalty to the High King is commendable and will be rewarded.”

After pausing for a few minutes to consult Fritz via thought-speak, I rose from my seat, removed one of the rings I had been given by Fritz as part of my royal ensemble and slid it onto the index finger of Moss' right hand.

“Lord James Moss, Ruler of Eutheria, I hereby name you Defender of the Realm for your faithfulness. When I am re-established upon my throne in Theria, you will be accorded the honors you deserve for your service.” Sitting back down, I sent a thank you to Fritz who had walked me through that little ceremony so I didn't mess things up.

Moss was speechless as he looked at the ring on his finger until he finally looked back at me with tears in his eyes. “Thank you, Sire, I am honored.”

Grinning wildly and winking I answered, “You are most welcome, now could you please pass the platter, I would like a bit more to eat.”

We talked about inconsequential things for the remainder of the meal but I could tell there was something else on Moss' mind that we hadn't already covered. Every time I thought he had mustered the courage to broach the subject, he would look down at his plate rather than say what he wanted. We were finished eating and I was about to leave the table when he finally said what was on his mind.

"Sire, I m-mean Alister," he stammered, "Lady Bronwyn and I were wondering if you would be so kind as to preside over our wedding before you leave to defeat Dimitri."

Stunned, I sat back in my chair. My first reaction was to say no, what did I know about marriage? I've never even had a girlfriend. But instead, I asked, "Are you sure?"

"Sire, we would be honored if you would do this for us. Lady

Bronwyn deserves so much better than me but for some reason, she has agreed to go through the process to become a fire drake and marry me. I don't deserve this honor after the way I ruined your parents' wedding and treated them so badly, but I beg this of you, for my Lady's sake."

"Uncle James, you don't need to keep bringing up what you did in the past. My parents have forgiven you; I've forgiven you and you have a chance to do things differently. Just so you're aware, I don't know what I'm doing, but am honored to preside over your wedding," I answered.

Gustav sent, *Fritz and Frieda will be able to help you with this. You will be fine.*

Is it wrong that I would rather have Aileene knock me out of the sky again than do this? I panicked.

"Thank you, Sire," Moss gushed, "Lady Bronwyn will be so pleased."

"Well, then," I said and rose from the table, "I'd better meet Aileene, Shelley and Bernie for a flying session. By the way, does she know about the whole 'we were made for each other' thing?"'

Both Moss and Gustav nodded. "I talked to her this morning while we were training," Gustav added.

"Great, this day gets better and better," I muttered as I left the room.

The sun was shining brightly overhead as I left the castle in search of my friends. The warmth of the sun made me want to turn into my dragon and bask in the heat for a few hours, but there were too many things to do.

"When am I going to find the time to learn how to preside over a wedding," I muttered while turning a corner and seeing my friends standing in an open field behind the castle.

My eyes were drawn to Aileene and all of the things that were pressing in on me fled when I looked at her. Even though nothing had changed since we had breakfast together, I now saw her in a new light. She was already cute to me, but now that I realized that we were true mates, my heart skipped a beat when I looked at her. She stood next to Bernie and was a couple of inches taller than her, so she was probably around six feet, three inches. Her rich auburn hair curled down her back. She was wearing a dark green doublet, black breeches and leather boots that came up to her knees. Her sword hung in a scabbard belted around her hips and she looked fierce. She turned towards me and smiled and it reminded me of sunlight shining through a break in storm clouds. Her sapphire-blue eyes twinkled as she looked at me and my steps faltered under the power of that look.

I hope you're not looking at me that way, Shelley snickered in my mind.

Oh, shut up, I sent and joined them on the lawn. "How was your training session with Gustav this morning?" I asked Aileene.

"Oh, it was quite invigorating," she answered.

"If by invigorating, you mean, being knocked to the ground repeatedly by Gustav and getting back up each time, then I agree with you," Bernie teased.

"Didn't you see the time I knocked him down as well?" Aileene protested.

"Are you talking about that time you ran at him, tripped over your own weapon and knocked him to the ground with your body?" Shelley asked.

"Yes," Aileene said proudly.

"That was some amazing strategy," Shelley laughed. Bernie and Aileene joined him.

"In my defense," Aileene answered, "I've never been taught to fight in human form. Lord Moss didn't think I would ever need to know how to do it."

I smiled at the three of them because it made me feel good that Bernie and Shelley fully accepted Aileene into our circle.

"Are you ready to show me your flying skills in dragon form?" I asked.

"I sure am," Aileene answered as she started to undo the buttons of her doublet.

Both Shelley and I instantly turned around so our backs were to Bernie and Aileene.

"What's wrong?" Aileene wondered.

"C'mon," Bernie laughed, "let's head away from the boys and I'll explain their reaction. This has nothing to do with you, we're not exactly used to the casual way most shifters accept nudity." I could hear the girls' voices recede into the distance.

"Some weather we're having," Shelley said as he looked up at the sky.

"Yep, it's a nice day for flying," I answered. We both laughed in embarrassment.

Gustav, I sent in a panic, *we need to make a thought medallion for Aileene, especially if we're going to train together as dragons. I'll feel much more comfortable if she doesn't have to take off her clothes before she becomes a dragon.*

I should have thought about that, Gustav sent, *we'll talk about it later.*

"I've got a lot to tell you and Bernie," I said to Shelley, "but that'll have to wait until Aileene and I do some flight training."

"That's cool," Shelley replied, "if it's okay with you, we'll hang out here and watch the two of you fly. It's peaceful here and it'll be nice to spend time together, as long as neither of you falls from the sky and crushes us, that is."

"We'll do our best," I muttered. "I've changed the plans for what I want to do. It would be nice for Aileene and me to fly and talk."

"Works for me, since you'll both be in your dragon forms, there's not much we can do to protect you. We'll be here waiting," Shelley said. After an instant he added, "Bernie and I like Aileene so far, she'll make a great addition to our team."

Before I had a chance to respond, I heard the girls come back.

Alister, you can turn around now, Aileene shyly sent.

The last time I saw Aileene in her dragon form, she was trying to kill me. This time I could appreciate her deadly beauty. When I turned to study Aileene's dragon I was struck by her beautiful iridescent green scales. While my scales transitioned from red to purple, her scales transitioned from lighter green near her underside to dark green along her back. She also had two golden stripes down her back and I realized her spikes would also be gold when she raised them.

I transformed into my dragon form so I could get a better idea of how we compared in size.

"How about a little warning next time, Stretch, you could have crushed me," I heard Shelley yell from the ground somewhere near my front feet. Aileene made a hissing/chuffing sound from her mouth that I realized was laughter.

Sorry, I sent absently but didn't take my gaze off Aileene. I slowly stalked around her and continued to study her dragon form. We were close to the same length, but while I was broader and more muscular, she was sleek and sinewy. Aileene followed the path of my investigation by swiveling her head on her elongated neck. Facing her again I moved my head towards her until we were snout to snout. I looked into her fathomless golden eyes and was mesmerized by them. Pleasure radiated from her and I'm sure she could feel the same thing coming from me. Aileene rubbed her muzzle along mine and I realized she was scent marking me.

Mine, she sent possessively.

Mine, I sent in response.

Aileene opened her mouth and gently nipped my neck. This took me by surprise and when I took a step back, she rammed herself into my chest, knocking me off balance. Before I could regain my footing, she launched herself into the air.

Bernie shouted something to me as I stood rooted to the spot watching her fly away. As I swiveled my head to look at Bernie, she shouted again, "She wants you to chase her, dummy," and both Shelley and Bernie laughed.

Launching myself into the air I swiftly caught up to Aileene.

Finally, she sent with humor, *I thought I would have to come back and issue you an invitation to join me.*

You took me by surprise, that's all, I sent.

I seem to do that a lot with you, she laughed at me, *we're supposed to be training, Alister, what do you have planned?*

Shaking my head to get my thoughts back on track it took me a few seconds to answer her. *Why don't we play a game of tag? I'll give you a ten-second head start and it's your job to keep me from tagging you with any part of my body. Once I tag you three times, you'll have to try to tag me three times, make sense?*

It does, Aileene answered.

Once you tag me three times, we'll switch up. We'll do this for an hour and in the end, the one with the most tags wins, deal?

Yes, she sent as she turned and whacked me with her tail hard enough across my snout to make my eyes water, *try to catch me.*

Tricky, I like it, I sent then closed my eyes to let them clear while hovering in place. After ten seconds I opened my eyes and the chase was on. It may not have been fair but while my eyes were closed, I checked to see if there was still a connection between us and there was; the strongest one I had sensed so far. With the connection to guide me, I used my powerful wings to catch up. Even though she was more lissome than me, I was able to keep up with her and tagged her quickly. The next two tags were relatively easy as well and then it was her turn.

Even though there were times over the next forty-five minutes I thought it would be fun to have her tag me, it was necessary that she work for it. Our contest was a display in acrobatics. Every time she would come close to me, I would do something to throw her off track and confound her attempts to catch me. She almost had me near the end of our time but when I turned into my human form it confused her so badly she ended up doing a somersault midair looking for me. Manifesting my wings and diving towards the ground I was able to fully escape the last attempt she made to tag me.

Shelley called time and the game was over.

Rather than transform back to my dragon self, I made my way close to Aileene and landed on her back. *Can I get a ride?* I sent and settled into a comfortable position near the base of her neck. I leaned forward and hugged her, *you did well.*

But I couldn't tag you, she answered.

True, but my guess is you've never trained like that before, have you?

No, I've only ever trained with drakes before and they aren't much of a challenge, she agreed.

Since you destroyed me the first time we met, let's say we're tied right now, I sent, lacing humor into my sending.

Agreed, I'm definitely in less pain than you were after our first encounter, she teased.

We laughed together and then I continued the conversation. *Lord Moss and Gustav told me some things about being a Royal Dragon over lunch I didn't know.*

Yeah, Gustav talked to me while we were training. It was surprising to hear what he had to say aloud, but to be honest I'd figured out much of that on my own over the years, Aileene admitted.

How does that make you feel? I asked.

Much better now that I've met you, Aileene sent, *and I look forward to spending more time together so we can really get to know each other.*

I feel the same way, in fact, on Earth when a guy wanted to spend more time with a girl he would ask her to go on a date, to get food or something. Would you like to go get some food? I asked.

CHAPTER NINE

I rolled onto my back, absolutely stuffed. Aileene had taken me about five miles from the castle to eat some sprìosh. These delicious creatures were the size of cows, looked like rats and their meat was somewhat spicy. They were delicious both cooked and raw and we tried them both ways. Looking at Aileene I couldn't help laughing.

What? She sent.

You've got a bit of sprìosh on your face, I snickered.

Was saving that for later, she sent and licked her face, slurping up the stray meat.

The sun felt warm on my scales and I was extremely relaxed. We had already told the others where we were and that we would be hanging out here so we could talk. I had to promise Shelley we would stay in dragon form so no one could harm us. Rolling onto my side so it was easier for me to look at her, I was surprised to see that she had curled around herself, with her head laying on her tail so she could look at me, too.

I already know that we hatched the same day, but who raised you? I asked.

Lord Moss, various other retainers, nurses and a dryad governess named Miss Birch, she sighed.

You mean, you didn't have a family of your own?

Sort of—Lord Moss did the best he could but he didn't treat me like a daughter. From what Gustav told me today, things should have been different and I should have grown up in Theria with you. Your family should have been my family.

That must have been hard, I mused.

Since I didn't know what I was missing until today, there's not really anything for me to compare it to. What happened? Why didn't anyone come from Theria to get me? she asked, sadness in her voice.

Don't you know what happened to the King and Queen?

No, the only thing anyone knew was about thirteen years ago all communications to and from Theria were cut off and nobody knew what happened. Envoys from the different kingdoms tried to get into Theria to find out what was going on, but there is some sort of shield around the kingdom and no one has been able to get in or out.

Wow, I breathed and proceeded to tell her about Dimitri, how he betrayed and killed my parents and about being separated from my shifter half for thirteen years. I described my life on Earth and the events leading to the discovery of who and what I really was. She asked a lot of questions when I also told her about the adventures we had in Middle Earth. It was difficult to explain why we called it that because she didn't have any reference to *The Lord of the Rings.* She really enjoyed hearing about our journey from Middle Earth to Eutheria and she asked me to describe, in great detail, every animal I ate along the way.

Feeling emboldened, I decided to share with her the dream I'd been having about my parents and how they might still be alive; but also how time was running out for them if I didn't find them soon. As I spoke, her eyes filled with tears and I could feel her sending comfort through our connection.

Alister, I'm so sorry that you had to go through that. I can't imagine how difficult it was to have your shifter half bound and your memories repressed, Aileene whispered in my mind.

To be honest, I didn't know what was missing until right before my halves were rejoined. I love being a dragon, and even though I've got the weight of being High King, I wouldn't trade it for anything in the world. There's just so much I don't know. If Dimitri hadn't done what he did, I would have had eighteen years of training up to this point to prepare me for my role. I've only shared this with my dad, but I feel like I'm making this up as I go along. This next thing is something I'm only sharing with you; I'm afraid I'm going to mess everything up.

Aileene looked at me with such compassion in her eyes that I teared up as well. She stretched her neck over to me and rubbed her muzzle on mine and licked one of the tears that had fallen down my face. It felt like the most natural thing in the world and gave me great comfort. The moment passed and Aileene leaned back and looked me in the eyes. Hers began to glow brighter and it looked like flames were flickering in their depths.

Alister, we've only met recently but An'Ceann made us for each other and our lives are intertwined in ways we don't understand. Neither of us is ready for this yet, but we are true mates and we will take the time we need until we are ready to be married. But you need to know this, your battles are my battles, your pain is my pain and your joy is my joy. Dimitri has stolen from both of us. He stole your parents, your training and the years you spent trapped in your human form. From me, he stole the years we would have spent growing up together to prepare us for this day. He also stole my family from me, the family I would've had if your parents hadn't died and you didn't have to go away. Your enemy is my enemy. Dimitri will die for his crimes. No one steals from a dragon, Aileene finished with a growl.

Rubbing my muzzle against hers I thanked An'Ceann for giving me such a fierce mate and partner. No matter what happened in the days ahead, I knew we would face it together.

Kingdom of Theria
Dimitri's Tent

Dimitri sat up in the dark, gasping, his heart pounding. Even though he knew it was a dream, he couldn't push the images from his mind. He had walked into the dining hall in his fortress to once again gloat over the sleeping forms of his former friends. They had delayed his victory by slipping into a hibernating sleep but he was certain they couldn't last much longer. Neither of them had anything to eat or drink for over thirteen years. As he was about to leave the room, he was shocked to see first Phillip's and then Beatrice's eyes open and they snarled at him. Both slowly rose to their feet and began to stalk towards him; he was completely paralyzed. Phillip opened his huge mouth and lunged at him. He fell backward and woke up.

After slowing his breathing, Dimitri laughed at himself and how he had been frightened by a dream. He sat in the dark, thinking about his plans when Phillip and Beatrice were dead once and for all. He also imagined what it would be like to crush the life out of Alister. It would be difficult, but not impossible because he would force Alister to change to human form by threatening the lives of those he must hold dear. The boy was more vulnerable in human form and Dimitri would use his fear against him. Even though the hatchling was a Royal Dragon, he wouldn't know what to do with the power at his disposal. Although Phillip and Beatrice didn't die the way he had planned, they hadn't been there to teach Alister the secrets of his heritage.

"Jeffrey," he shouted into the night.

Moments later, Jeffrey came running in with a light. "Yes, my lord?" he asked.

He rose from his bed, took two steps towards Jeffrey and struck him across the face with the back of his hand. "When I call you, I expect you to answer me immediately. Do you understand?"

Jeffrey bowed low and groveled. "I am sorry, m'lord, it will not happen again."

"No, it won't, or we will see how much pain your wife can endure before she curses your name. I have a job for you."

Jeffrey paled at the threat. "What is your bidding?"

"I have been too lenient on the fools I left behind at the fortress. You will leave immediately and lock everyone in the dungeon without food and water. I will be victorious in the coming battle, but if not, then no one else will survive either. You are fortunate that I allowed your family to travel with me so you won't have to lock them away as well. I am most magnanimous, am I not?"

"You are, my lord," Jeffrey said with his forehead on the ground.

"Then be off, do my will then return. Any delay will be unfortunate for your wife and children. I fear I have too many mouths to feed as it is and may decide to reduce the drain on my resources. You have two days to perform this task and return."

"But, my lord, it took us almost a full day of hard marching to get here to begin with," Jeffrey pleaded.

"Then you better hurry, be off with you." Dimitri laughed evilly.

"It will be as you say," Jeffrey said. He burst through his clothes as he transformed into a massive polar bear and ran out of the tent.

Eutheria

Alister

As I sat at the table eating my breakfast last night's dream replayed through my mind. In most ways, it was the same as always but instead of flying over fields with my parents we flew over snow-covered plains towards an imposing fortress on a hill. Gustav would know if this was a real location or just my imagination. My heart hurt when I thought about how bad my mother looked in the dream. Her despair was a tangible thing and I woke up sobbing.

Aileene placed her hand on mine and I was startled out of my dark thoughts. She gave me strength and comfort from that small touch and I was grateful. Looking at her smile, I caught Shelley and Bernie grinning at me from across the table. It was impossible to ignore their stares, especially with Shelley waggling his eyebrows so rapidly I was afraid they would jump off his face.

"So, Alister, what do you have planned for today?" Shelley asked innocently; I wasn't buying his act.

"After breakfast, I need to meet with Gustav to help him create a thought medallion for Aileene," I answered.

"I thought Gustav didn't have enough access to magic here to create one," Bernie countered.

"We figured out a way for me to open a very small gate to Middle Earth, about the size of a baseball, which will allow Gustav to draw the magic necessary to create the medallion. This opening won't weaken the other gates and I'm pretty sure Dimitri can't find a way to use this to his advantage. It only needs to stay open for five minutes or so."

"That's pretty impressive, Alister," Aileene commented and I blushed.

"Anyway," Shelley continued, "what do you have planned after that?"

"After that, I need to meet with Fritz to figure out how to preside over a wedding, then I'll work with the army again to perfect our takedown technique," I answered.

"And then?" Bernie asked, getting into the game.

"And then, lunch?" I hedged as I glanced sideways at Aileene.

"Sure, lunch, and then what?" Shelley smiled.

"And then, oh yeah, and then Aileene and I will train for a bit. Just to make sure, she's ready for the upcoming battle," I answered.

Aileene beamed at me and I felt like there were a thousand butterflies in my stomach.

"That'll be nice," Shelley grinned, "don't you want to know what Bernie and I will be doing until we meet up again this afternoon?"

"Not really," I grumbled, "but I have a feeling you'll tell me whether I want you to or not."

"That's right, I will," Shelley teased. "Bernie and I will be filling Aileene in on the years she missed being stuck in this castle. We'll help her get to know the real you."

My face froze in horror as I thought about what that could possibly mean.

Bernie chuckled as she added, "Let me translate what Shelley is trying to say since your brain has evidently shut down. We're going to tell Aileene all the embarrassing stories about you we can remember."

"And if we can't remember them all, we'll probably make some up," Shelley laughed. "C'mon girls, we've got a lot to do today," Shelley said as the three of them stood.

Aileene leaned over and kissed me on the cheek, "Don't worry, I'll only believe half of what they tell me," she said with a smile.

I was still sitting stunned when the three of them left the room, laughing.

The next two days passed in a blur of activity. I learned how to create a thought medallion, crammed information about how to preside over a wedding and honed our takedown strategy with our army, which now numbered about five thousand troops.

Shelley and I held an epic wrestling match where I managed to put Shelley in his place for sharing my most embarrassing moments with Aileene while showing her my wrestling skills at the same time. Shelley and I may have also knocked down a tree or two, but we promised to replant those along with all the others that were destroyed when I fell from the sky. We also discovered that Bernie was better at swordplay than me when we sparred; she soundly defeated me nine times out of ten.

My favorite part of every day was flying with Aileene. We would always start with flying by ourselves and then would train with Shelley on my back and Bernie on hers. We spent hours each afternoon chasing one another through the sky and learning new aerial maneuvers. Even though the battle was always on our mind, the last few hours of each day was really more about playing together than actual training for the fight, Gustav took care of that with his morning lessons.

Aileene would work with Gustav in her human form for a few hours and then have her shift so she could train with various shifters in their natural forms. The idea was to help Aileene learn how to subdue enemy combatants without killing them. Bernie was always on hand to engage Aileene in mock battle but also to heal anyone when the training got too vigorous. According to Bernie, Aileene was a beautiful, destructive force with an eagerness for battle; I wish I could have watched her train.

The last thing we did before going back to the castle was fly to

Aileene's favorite spot and eat a sprìosh or two as a snack before dinner. Shelley tried one and thought it was delicious. Bernie contented herself with grazing on the grass while in her unicorn form. She told us later it was an amazing blend with hints of spice, clover and lemon; we took her word for it.

The evening before the battle we gathered in the throne room for the wedding. The room had been transformed to resemble a sunny glade. Lights hung from the ceiling and replicated the warmth and light of a midsummer's day. The walls were festooned with flowers and evergreen branches and the floor was covered in grass which had been cut from a nearby meadow and rolled out like a carpet. There were musicians staged in the corner with stringed instruments and they played lively music. Uncle James and I were standing side by side, under an archway made of woven willow branches and blooming flowers. We faced the closed doors through which Lady Bronwyn would enter the room to start the ceremony.

It was amazing how much the room looked like the outdoors and I asked him why we hadn't held the ceremony outside.

"Usually we would," he said quietly, "but we wanted to get married before you left tomorrow and it will probably start raining at any time."

A rumble of thunder sounded in the distance so I said, "Good call. How do you feel?"

He answered, "Nervous, excited, grateful and ashamed."

"I get the, nervous, excited and grateful, but why ashamed?" I asked.

"I can't help thinking about Albert and Fiona's wedding and how my selfishness ruined their day. I know she won't do it, but it would serve me right if she interrupted today to get back at me."

How much longer until Lady Bronwyn makes her entrance? I sent to Gavin, her father, who would be escorting her down the aisle.

We're almost ready, about two minutes, he sent, *is anything wrong?*

Not at all, I just need to say something to my uncle before he's distracted by his bride-to-be, I answered.

Just let us know when you're ready, he replied.

"First of all," I whispered, although everyone in the room would hear what we were saying if they chose to listen in, "Mom would never do that to Lady Bronwyn even if she thought you deserved it. Secondly, she's decided to forgive you so she wouldn't do that to you either. Lastly, she's happy for you both. Not only that you're getting married, but also that you've gotten over your prejudice."

"Falling in love with Bronwyn has certainly helped," he replied. We looked at Mom and she stuck her tongue out at Uncle James to make him laugh. "I still can't believe Bronwyn was willing to transform into a fire drake to be with me. I don't deserve her love."

"From what I'm learning about that kind of love, we don't deserve it but we can keep working on making it better every day," I replied as I looked over at Aileene and she smiled at me. *We're ready.* I sent to Gavin and nodded to the musicians.

The song they had been playing faded to silence and after a slight pause, they began to play something stirring and upbeat. The doors opened and I heard James suck in a breath next to me when he saw Bronwyn in her wedding gown. She was radiant and the look she gave her future husband was full of love and anticipation.

Gavin was in his manticore form as he walked down the aisle with his daughter. James asked him to escort Bronwyn this way so everyone would know she had given up being a manticore to marry him. Her love for him really had broken down his old prejudices. The crowd rose when the doors opened and they tracked the progress of the bride and her father as they walked down the aisle. They stopped a few feet away and stood facing us.

"Who gives this woman to be married to this man?" I asked.

Gavin transformed back into his human form to answer me. Unfortunately, he didn't have any clothes to transform with him but at least he was wearing the cloak he had on as a manticore. One day I would get used to the casual way shifters treated nudity.

"Her mother and I do," Gavin replied, his voice rough with emotion. He kissed his daughter on the cheek and he placed her right hand in James' left and joined his wife in the front row. James and Bronwyn turned to face me.

"Please be seated," I said, and waited while everyone settled.

Looking over the crowd I saw my parents sitting with each other, holding hands. I thought about all the things Fritz and Frieda had taught me about weddings over the past couple of days and took a deep breath. Looking at James and Bronwyn I began.

"We are here today because you two want to join your lives in marriage. There have been a lot of preparations to make today special and everything looks wonderful. However, this ceremony will only last one day but your marriage will last a lifetime so you want to keep putting effort into your marriage daily. I don't have any personal knowledge of marriage, yet, but have learned some things by watching my parents. If you want to get good at something, you have to work on it, and that includes marriage. My parents do little things to work on theirs each day. One example of this, whenever Dad goes to get himself a drink or snack, he asks Mom if she wants something, too. Mom does the same thing for Dad.

"When they disagree about something and argue, I've heard them not only apologize, but also ask the other person to forgive them for what they did or for their poor attitude. They laugh together, support each other and are interested in what the other person is interested in as well. Just ask them later about sweatpants. Dad loves them, and Mom loves to buy them for him, the crazier the better." Our friends laughed because they knew what I was talking about and everyone else laughed because my friends did.

"No, I don't personally know what it's like to be married, but everything I do know, I've learned by watching them. Find someone else who has a marriage you admire, ask them what they do to make it great, then follow their example."

I looked over at Fritz and Frieda because I had gone completely away from what they had taught me to do but they smiled and nodded approvingly at me. The rest of the ceremony went according to plan and it wasn't long before Moss and Bronwyn were married and I was introducing the new couple to the audience.

"It is my honor to introduce to you for the first time, Lord and Lady, James and Bronwyn Moss. May you rule Eutheria wisely in the ways of An'Ceann and under my authority as High King of all Theria."

The crowd cheered as the happy couple kissed again and made their way down the aisle.

Dinner was delicious and the celebration looked like it would still be going on for hours when Aileene, Bernie and Shelley approached the table where I was sitting. Even though Bernie and Shelley were my Knights, since I was under the protection of Lord Moss and his retinue they had freedom to sit elsewhere. They chose to sit in a corner with Aileene and try to make me laugh by sending ridiculous thoughts my way whenever I was talking to a Eutherian noble. I glared good-naturedly at my friends as they stood before me.

"Well, this party's been a blast," Shelley began, "but we've got other things to do. We're outta here."

"Yep, we've got a big day ahead of us tomorrow so we'll take our leave, goodnight Sire," Bernie added.

Wilting in my seat because while I really wanted to go with my friends, I figured it would be proper for me to stay here until the festivities wound down.

"Enjoy the rest of your evening, I'll see you in the morning," I answered with a grimace.

"I have a message from Lord and Lady Moss, I was asked to deliver to you," Aileene said.

"Oh, what is it?" I asked.

"Lord and Lady Moss thank you for the kindness you showed them by presiding over their wedding and respectfully request, and I quote, 'please go with your friends, your moping face is ruining the mood,' close quote." Aileene beamed at me.

Whipping my head around to where the happy couple were sitting I saw they were laughing at me as they waved me off. I jumped out of my chair and took off with my friends before anyone could change their mind.

A King never runs from a room, Frieda sent to me, *but a fast walk is permissible, Sire.*

Thanks, I sent back as we hurried from the room. Shelley led the way as we walked to a part of the castle I hadn't been to before. I didn't really care where we were going, it just felt great to spend time with my friends. Shelley and Bernie walked in front of us, holding hands. I tentatively reached towards Aileene and she put her hand in mine and we twined fingers. I felt like I was walking on air. We stopped in front of a closed door and Shelley looked at me seriously.

"We've got a surprise for you, but I don't want you to freak out when we show you. Can you keep your cool?"

"Sure, you know me," I said.

"We do, that's why I'm asking. Bernie thinks you'll be able to, but I'm betting against you. Do me proud my friend, win me this bet," Shelley grinned.

"Whatever," I mumbled.

Shelley opened the door with a magician's flourish, "Ta-da!"

I walked into the room and looked around. There was a large, leather couch in the center of the room facing a wall. It took me a little while to realize there was a small, flat-screen TV mounted to the wall with a bunch of wires running from it. Under the TV there was a cabinet with a Blu Ray player on top of it. Sitting next to the player was *The Lord of the Rings* Blu Ray boxed set extended edition.

"What? How did you get this here? Oh, man, this is so cool! Aileene, you're going to love these movies, this is awesome, I can't believe you guys managed this. You're great!" I gushed.

"You win," Bernie muttered to Shelley as she pushed me into the room.

"How did you get the TV and Blu Ray player here? How did you hook it up?" I continued.

Aileene laughed, grabbed my arm and pulled me to the couch to sit next to her. "Your parents brought the TV and player with them from Earth and carried them on your journey here. It's a good thing they weren't in your pack or they would have been destroyed when you crashed," she said as she squeezed my arm.

"I still need to see the crash site," I said.

"It's a thing of beauty," Shelley laughed.

"Anyway," Bernie continued, "the castle already has electricity so we just had to get your dad to help with the wiring so we wouldn't blow up the equipment. We've been watching movies the last two nights but wanted to wait for tonight to start LOTR."

"What have you been watching, and why wasn't I invited?" I complained.

"We watched *Jurassic Park 1 & 2*, and you weren't invited because you were busy doing kingly stuff," Shelley answered.

"I really like the T-Rex," Aileene said.

"She kept cheering every time the dinosaur took out another human," Bernie smiled.

Aileene narrowed her gaze and looked intently at me. "I was rooting for the parents to find their lost baby. If someone stole our child, anyone who had anything to do with its capture would be fried to a crisp."

I was warmed by Aileene's mention of 'our child,' and smiled at her enthusiasm and the effort my friends had put into this surprise. I hugged her and said, "Thanks guys, I appreciate this."

"No problem," Shelley waved me off.

"How are you feeling about tomorrow?" Bernie asked.

Shrugging, I answered, "I'm worried about trying to keep everyone alive but mostly I'm anxious to see if my dreams really mean anything or not. I don't want to get my hopes up, but tomorrow we could find out my parents are alive."

"Did Gustav give you any more insight into your dream?" Aileene asked as she put her arm around my shoulders.

"Yes, he told me the location I described was Dimitri's fortress. My parents took me to visit when I was three but I don't remember that," I answered.

"What are we going to do about it?" Bernie asked.

It hit me that my friends were with me, no matter what, and we would find out the truth together. Swallowing the lump in my throat, I answered, "After I defeat Dimitri, I'm going to try to open a gate to the place in my dream and search the fortress until we find the truth about my parents. I would like it if you all come with me."

"Of course, Alister," Aileene commented, "where you go, I go."

"Yep," Shelley added and then his face brightened as he got an idea. "We'll all go. We should call ourselves The Fellowship of the Dream."

Bernie and I groaned at the pun but Aileene looked confused. "Don't worry, you'll understand after we watch the movie, and then you'll groan, too," I said.

As I settled back on the couch, Aileene nestled herself against my side and Shelley got the movie started. He and Bernie were on one end of the couch and we were on the other. I couldn't imagine anything better than watching my favorite movie with my favorite people. Tomorrow would be hard but I also knew that it would be the end of Dimitri's reign of evil and the beginning of something better.

CHAPTER TEN

Morning had broken when we gathered in the field the next day. Even though we had stayed up late watching the movie, I was energized for what was to come. Looking out at the troops in their formation, I marveled at how dangerous they looked standing on the field. Aileene and I were flanked by Bernie and Shelley as we walked to where the generals were standing.

"Good morning, Sire, Lady Aileene, Sirs Einhorn and Arktos," General Arktos greeted us when we joined them.

"Good morning, Dad," Shelley grinned as he hugged his father.

McIntyre laughed as Stavros ruffled Shelley's hair affectionately and said, "You're incorrigible, my boy."

"Yep," Shelley laughed, "I must get it from Mom."

"Are we ready?" I asked.

"As ready as we're going to be," General McIntyre responded, "but as my friend Stavros reminded me, the best battle plans never survive first contact with the enemy."

"We plan the best we can, then adapt as necessary," Stavros continued, "the way battles have always been fought. Sire, I know you want to minimize casualties as much as possible, but it will be impossible to save everyone. I know you well enough to say you will want to blame yourself for every death today. However, I want you to remember that Dimitri is responsible for everything that has happened or will take place because of his treachery. Please take care of what only you can take care of and let the rest of us play our roles."

Hugging Stavros I thanked him for his kind words. When General McIntyre gave me a strange look, I gave him a hug as well and laughed at the startled expression on his face.

"Guess I'd better take my place at the front and address the troops. Take care of yourself; we will be victorious today," I said and hugged Aileene.

"Of course we will," she answered fiercely, "no one stands against The Fellowship of the Dreams."

I groaned at the pun while Shelley high-fived both Aileene and Bernie.

"Don't ask," I said to the confused generals, "it only encourages them."

Moving to a space large enough to hold my dragon, I transformed then Bernie and Shelley climbed onto my back. We weren't planning on any fancy maneuvers so they didn't need the saddles today and we had been practicing them riding on my back without them. We took off and made our way towards the front of the army. Landing, I turned to face the troops and broadcast my thoughts to everyone.

Today we bring an end to the tyranny brought about by Dimitri. He has used his power to cause death, destruction and has oppressed those weaker than himself. My Kingdom is built on the principle, Protect the Weak; anyone who follows me agrees to make this part of their lives as well. Today, we will Protect the Weak and rescue them from their oppressors. Who's with me?

The roar from over five thousand voices was deafening. *Today we fight, today we free the oppressed, today we will be victorious,* I shouted and connected to the shifters surrounding me. My power reservoir had doubled in size over the past three days and was brimming with energy. I turned away from the troops and concentrated on opening a gate from this field to the fairgrounds in Theria. The gate opened in front of me but there was some kind of purple barrier blocking our way forward. I studied the barrier and recognized it held energy signatures from my royal parents. Lifting my right leg as high as I could, I bent my head down to bite down on my leg to draw blood to the surface.

Flinging my blood at the barrier caused it to disappear with a flash of white light. My leg had already healed by the time the barrier dropped but I licked off the remaining blood before standing again. The moment the barrier disappeared I felt tens of thousands of new connections attach themselves to the ones I had open with my army. I sent a sense of strength down each new connection and was rewarded with a pulse of energy coupled with a feeling of relief. If I concentrated long enough, I would've been able to pinpoint where each of the shifters were who connected to me. Some of the connections were weaker than others so I sent more energy down those lines and could feel them strengthen again.

Mentally keeping track of my energy reservoir I was able to estimate that I had sent a quarter of my energy down those weaker lines. As before there were two that seemed to take more energy than the others. Unfortunately, I had to cut those off before they drained too much from me.

Forward, I shouted and launched myself into the air to lead the way but landed shortly after crossing the barrier so I could monitor the energy exchange. By expanding my connections I was able to draw a small amount of power from each line, except the weakest ones, to refill my reserves. This took about thirty minutes and by then all our troops had arrived on the field. It took very little effort for me to close the gate behind us, almost like an afterthought.

Generals, are we ready? I sent.

Yes, Sire, they replied.

Mom, Dad, are you prepared for your part of the battle? I asked.

You can count on us, son, Mom sent.

Fritz, Frieda, what's your status?

We have a contingent of healers ready to assist with casualties, Frieda answered.

Aileene—I started but she interrupted me.

It's cute that you worry, but no need. I've climbed high enough that I cannot be seen from the ground and have started making my way north. I will engage Dimitri from behind and keep him occupied until you get there, my mate, Aileene sent and I could feel the thrill of battle from Aileene coursing through our connection.

Good hunting, I sent and then addressed the army as a whole again, *as silent as we can, we march.*

It takes time to move thousands of people five miles. The majority of our army marched in their human forms because we figured that would be the easiest way to subdue the enemy. The exception was our far-seeing flyers like the eagles, hawks, griffins, and drakes. They would tell me whenever they spotted enemy scouts and I would quickly force them into their human forms and our troops would subdue them. Although there were injuries, some of them quite serious, we were able to capture each of these scouts without fatalities. Once they were bound, we would leave them where they were so the medical team could take charge of them and place them on the medical wagons we brought with us.

When we were about a mile away from where we would engage Dimitri, I dropped back behind our army and settled on the ground. The generals decided it would be best for me to walk the rest of the way, to avoid being spotted in the air. Based on the amount of complaining from Shelley, I surmised this wasn't the most comfortable mode of travel. Chuckling to myself, I might have bounced around a bit more than necessary until I heard Bernie start to complain as well.

Hmmm—I guess you shouldn't have told Aileene about the time in first grade when I laughed so hard in class I wet my pants, I sent.

"Okay, we're even, but, if you don't stop, I'll probably throw up on your back...again," Bernie grumbled.

I smoothed out my gait right away.

Sire, I can see the enemy troops, Erich, one of the eagles sent to me. He was our high-altitude scout and was above the clouds to avoid being seen. *I'm not able to get an accurate count but it looks like our forces are fairly evenly matched.*

Thank you, I sent to him and then addressed everyone else. *The enemy will come into sight as we crest the next ridge. Our numbers are fairly evenly matched but we have the element of surprise on our side. They won't expect us to engage them in human form and they will be disoriented when I force them to shift to their human forms and keep them that way. Lady Aileene will engage Dimitri until I can join the fight. Remember our training. For Theria!*

We began to run and our army flowed up the hill like a river of destruction. Once again I took to the air but only soared fifteen feet above the ground.

Once we reached the top of the hill, I settled down and concentrated on connecting with the enemy soldiers. *Now,* I cried and spied Aileene diving towards an unsuspecting Dimitri. Reaching deep into my reservoir of power I mentally shouted, *shift!*

Every enemy combatant dropped to the ground as a human while many also tumbled from the sky. Our troops in the lead kept running past the downed soldiers, their job was to start subduing the enemy from the back of their lines and work their way towards our front line. Dimitri was left standing and he bellowed with rage as he watched his defeat at the hands of our army. I had to concentrate to keep the shifters incapacitated so they could be bound without too much trouble. I was enraged when Dimitri skewered one of our soldiers who had gotten too close to him. He stabbed through both my soldier and his at the same time, he didn't care about his people. Aileene reached him at that point and I knew he had been taken out of the battle.

Even though I was able to turn the enemy shifters into their human forms, it took a tremendous amount of energy to keep them that way. Half of the enemy were bound on the ground but there were groups of enemy soldiers who had shifted again and were fighting fiercely. Hundreds of combatants broke out of the nearby tree line and charged towards our soldiers who were focused on binding the ones on the ground.

We have enemies incoming from the west, I broadcast to my generals.

Albert, Fiona, take them down! General Arktos shouted.

I watched in horror as the incoming soldiers tore through my people like they were made of tissue paper and felt the pain of loss for each shifter whose life force was snuffed out. Mom and Dad roared out of the sky and crashed into the enemy, and I could hear the sound of bodies breaking from the collision. Drakes aren't as large as Royal Dragons but they are still formidable fighters. Mom was a terror as she whipped her tail around knocking down enemy soldiers while using her teeth and claws to incapacitate any of those close to her. Dad mirrored her actions but was slower than Mom and I watched a huge bear rake his claws down Dad's side drawing blood. Mom reacted to Dad's bellow of pain and lashed out at the bear with her wing and sent it flying to land in a heap of bloody fur. My parents were swarmed by the enemy and were overwhelmed by the large number of soldiers attacking them.

As much as I wanted to go to my parents and help them in their fight, it was my job to keep as many shifters in human form as possible so we could continue to subdue them. There was an explosion of movement where the enemy had piled onto my mom and shifters went flying in all directions. She streaked over to where my dad was dealing with his own group and waded into the fray. Between the two of them they managed to get those shifters off Dad and renewed their efforts in the attack. Although my parents were wounded, bloody and their wings were in tatters, they overpowered those they battled and soon their enemies were either unconscious or dead.

Dad collapsed in exhaustion and Mom stood over his prone form radiating menace towards anyone who tried to come close to him.

Are you okay? How's Dad? I mentally shouted to my mom.

We're fine Alister, don't worry about us, Mom sent me comforting thoughts, *I'll call the healers for your dad and the other wounded, you focus on what you have to do.*

Sire, it's time, General McIntyre sent, *open the gate to Middle Earth.*

Shortly after we came through the gate to Theria I opened another gate to Middle Earth and sent Gustav, Miriam and Wu through to organize the shifters on the other side so they could help in the fight against Dimitri. We didn't know exactly how long it would take for us to get to this point of the battle but wanted our people to be ready to join us the moment the gate was opened. We estimated that we would only get about fifty fighters from that group but they would be well rested, have weapons at the ready and would help finish the fight.

It took me a moment to detach from the shifters who were incapacitated and use that energy to open the gate to Middle Earth. With a mighty roar, our people rushed through the gate and joined the battle. Miriam led a group of bears, Wu led a group of cats, Gustav flew through the gate leading a group of flying shifters. Askari, Shujaa and Mkali were the last to pass through the gate and were firing arrows at the enemy before they finished crossing. The moment they passed the opening, I shut the gate so none of Dimitri's soldiers could escape to Middle Earth. The newcomers were so ferocious in their attack they quickly overwhelmed the soldiers who were still standing and we once again gained the upper hand. Gathering my power, I sent another pulse of energy with the command to change and shifted those who were still fighting into their human forms and they were captured without further incident.

Among the bound combatants, there were wounded and dying shifters lying on the ground. The medical teams were racing towards the battlefield to assist those who could still be saved but for some it was too late. My anger grew with every death. Aileene was attacking Dimitri from the air and it was like watching a cat playing with a mouse. Her role was to keep Dimitri occupied so he wouldn't pay attention to the battlefield and she was doing it wonderfully. The all-clear signal went up from each battalion.

General McIntyre sent, *the field is yours, Sire.*

Drawing energy from each of the enemy shifters I was connected to, I refilled my reservoir. This served to replenish my energy which also gave me the strength to keep the enemy shifters subdued. Concentrating on the thought medallion on Dimitri's chest I was able to see the magic surrounding the gift he had received from my parents when he was part of their Inner Circle. Since working with Gustav, not only did I know how to make a thought medallion, but also how to destroy one. Just as Dimitri struck at Aileene with his lance, I sent a pulse of energy and destroyed his medallion. The lance hit Aileene in the chest and shattered while at the same time Dimitri was thrown to the ground by the force of the medallion exploding.

Dimitri scrambled to his feet and I forced him to shift into his human form. Aileene picked him up in her claws and carried him to the middle of the battlefield. Gliding off the hill I met Aileene and Dimitri where Bernie and Shelley slid off my back.

CHAPTER ELEVEN

P*lease make sure he doesn't leave,* I sent to Aileene and looked at Dimitri. He was the source of so much pain, death and destruction and we had stopped him. I narrowed my eyes and growled at him while showing my fangs and taking a step forward. He tried to take a step back but Aileene was pressed against him so he couldn't move. Transforming into my human self while taking another step brought me a little bit closer. Memories of him smiling at me acting like a loving uncle played in my mind, but now I knew that had all been a lie. Hardening the skin on my back and chest, I purposefully turned away from him. As expected, he attacked and I felt something hit my back. It didn't hurt me but I saw a knife bounce once as it hit the ground. Aileene growled at his action and I knew she was an instant from biting off Dimitri's head, but I held up my hand to stop her.

"Aileene, he acted as expected but he did me no harm. He will be dealt with in due time, please make sure he witnesses what is about to happen to all his schemes," I said walking away from where they were standing.

Making my way to the place where I had already opened the gate to Middle Earth, I waved my hand and opened another, wider one. We all saw the camp and our remaining people waiting on the other side.

Leaving the gate open I continued turning in a circle to look at all the shifters who were on the battlefield.

Raising my voice and projecting my thoughts at the same time, I declared, "Come witness the judgment of Dimitri Frost Giant and see justice served on him. Those of you who were forced to flee your homes are given this right in recompense for the years Dimitri stole from you. A warning to those of you who served in Dimitri's army of rebellion, we will discover which of you served willingly and which of you served out of fear for your families. Either way, you will bear witness to the justice we will levy today. Each of you will also be tried and judged at a time of our choosing."

After my proclamation, I waited until everyone had either moved on their own or were dragged into position by their captors. While this was happening I was giving commands and receiving reports by thought-speak.

Do not worry about your possessions on Middle Earth, you will be able to retrieve them later, I sent and closed the gate after the last shifter had joined us. Turning around, I once again faced a naked, bloody and dirty Dimitri.

Did he try to escape? I asked Aileene.

She nodded and released a bit of smoke from her nostrils, *as you see the coward didn't get very far.*

Well done, I sent to Aileene and she preened under my praise.

"Dimitri, breaker of oaths, betrayer of friends, hope crusher, thief and murderer, you stand condemned before everyone gathered here today. Do you have anything to say on your behalf?" I asked and looked at this person who had caused so much pain, death and destruction.

He sneered as he answered, "I have no need to defend my actions. The strong rule the weak, as it should be. I killed your parents, who were true dragons, and took over as is the right of the mighty. Who do you think you are, hatchling? Who are you to condemn me?"

"By your own argument, I condemn you because I'm stronger than you and have shown that by defeating you and your army," I answered.

"You may have defeated my army but it is this female dragon who bested me. Fight me as a man and I will prove that you are unfit to rule," Dimitri shouted.

"There is nothing to prove to you, betrayer. My rule as High King isn't due to the strength of my dragon but because I choose to serve An'Ceann. He has given me the rule over all Theria," I stated calmly which seemed to infuriate Dimitri even more.

"Fight me," Dimitri shouted again, "I claim the right of rule by combat."

What's that? I asked Fritz and Frieda.

Frieda responded, *This is part of our ancient history and not anything that we've recognized for thousands of years. Dimitri is claiming that he is a ruler and as such is challenging your right to rule. You don't have to agree to this, Sire, Dimitri already violated any claim to honorable combat when he threw the knife at your back.*

And if I don't? I asked.

There may be some who question your right to rule and it could lead to violence amongst the other rulers across the planet, Fritz responded.

"Very well," I answered, "I accept your challenge. Please bring him a sword and some clothing."

"You must stay in human form, you cannot transform into your dragon," Dimitri hissed.

Nodding in agreement, I asked everyone to step back. Shelley handed my sword to me and after Dimitri was dressed Bernie handed a sword to him.

If he harms you, I will bite him in half, Aileene growled.

I laughed at her words which infuriated Dimitri even more and he charged, swinging wildly at my head. I ducked under the stroke and used my left hand to punch Dimitri on his right side, which he left unprotected. He staggered, but then regained his fighting stance and started using his sword properly. While Dimitri had centuries more practice fighting than me, I was pretty sure he hadn't faced a true opponent for years and wasn't used to fighting someone larger than him. Even though Dimitri was huge in his frost giant form, he was smaller than me by five inches in his human form.

"It was a pleasure watching your parents die," Dimitri said as he started circling towards the right looking for an opening. He was hoping to make me angry with his words which would cause me to make a mistake. I lunged at him as though his words had scored a hit and he pivoted on one leg to try to strike me while I was off balance. Anticipating his move I once again parried his strike and hit him in the face with my left hand, shattering his nose. Even though he was obviously in pain, he was still fast enough to bring his sword down and slash it across my left thigh. He scored a deep cut but I hopped back fast enough that I avoided losing my leg to his strike.

He was off balance and I brought my sword up to slice him across his chest with the tip. We backed off from each other and began to circle one another once again. Our enhanced healing ability kicked in and soon our wounds stopped leaking blood. We moved back towards each other and our swords rang in one continuous sound as our blows struck faster and faster. He wounded me, I wounded him and still we kept attacking one another. Dimitri was fighting for his life, but I was fighting for the lives of every shifter on the battlefield. Neither of us were willing to give ground to the other,but the wounds we were receiving were starting to take a toll on our bodies. Dimitri stepped too close to me and I delivered a vicious kick to his kneecap.

He bellowed his rage and used both hands to chop and slash at me with his sword. Dancing out of his way, I continued to block and parry his strikes as they came close to me. He began to swing wildly and I saw my opening. Stepping up to him, I blocked his sword with mine and stopped his swing cold. Clinching in the middle, I slid my blade up his towards the hilt of his sword and held it there, neither of us gaining an advantage over the other. Using my height and weight, I pressed in on him and he began to bow backwards under the added pressure. Using a move Bernie taught me when we were sparring, I dipped my hand and got the guard of my sword behind his and twisted my wrist to the right. Dimitri's sword went flying. He grabbed both my hands with his, smashed his forehead into my nose, threw himself backwards, used my own momentum against me and kicked me over his head.

I hit the ground hard and rolled to my right when I heard a warning shout. Dimitri had transformed into his frost giant form and was trying to stomp the life out of me while I lay on the ground. My eyes were still watering from when Dimitri smashed my nose and I was trying to blink rapidly to clear my vision. Dimitri landed a kick to my side which lifted me off the ground and sent me flying. I landed heavily and tried to get up. Sensing movement to my left, I was able to deflect Dimitri's kick and scrambled to my feet. Even though I could destroy him easily in my dragon form it was important for me to defeat the twenty-foot frost giant in my human form instead. Rushing over to where his sword lay on the ground I grabbed it and now had two swords to work with.

Dimitri began to hurl bolts of ice at me from a distance and while I managed to deflect most of them, some of them got through and I was dealing with gashes on my arms and legs. My chest and back were still covered with hardened dragon scales so he wasn't able to pierce anything vital, but my wounds were starting to slow me down. I was tempted to use my fire on the ice, but didn't want to use my dragon powers so openly. If I stayed on the defensive, sooner or later Dimitri would wear me down and cause some real damage to my body. Dimitri bellowed with rage each time I blocked one of his attacks and I was growing more concerned that he'd become so frustrated that he'd harm people in the crowd with these bolts of ice.

Diving to my right, I rolled and started running at Dimitri. My move caught him off guard so I gained a slight reprieve from the deadly ice bolts. Using my considerable speed, I continued on and shouted at him with my mind and dodged his attacks as I drew closer.

You sealed your fate when you betrayed the King and Queen and it's time for you to pay for your crimes. After you're dead, we will go to your fortress and free everyone we find there, including my parents.

Dimitri's eyes widened at my statement and he created an ice lance to try to skewer me with.

You have been judged and found guilty. All your schemes have failed, I sent.

Shouting, "Now you face justice," I ducked between Dimitri's legs and thrust both swords backwards to slice the Achilles tendons on both his legs. He bellowed in pain and began to fall forward because his feet couldn't bear his weight any longer. As he was falling, I pivoted and jumped on his back just as he hit the ground. Before he could make a move, I ran up the length of his body and plunged both swords into the back of his neck and with a scissor move removed his head. Dimitri was dead.

Without sparing another look at his lifeless body I sat down heavily while thousands of voices were raised in celebration.

Aileene, still in dragon form, knocked me flat on the ground with her snout and then held me down with her foot.

How badly are you hurt? She sent to me as she narrowed her eyes and moved her head to within inches of my face.

Smiling at her, I answered, "I'm mostly healed but would like to get up now."

She growled but moved her foot and let me stand. Holding up my hands for silence, I addressed those closest to me. "We're now going to Dimitri's fortress and release any prisoners he may be holding there."

Bernie and Shelley walked up to me holding a bruised and bloody man. He was being supported by my Knights but he dropped to his knees as soon as he got close to me. Aileene growled loudly but I sent soothing thoughts to her and she subsided.

"Who is this?" I asked.

"He claims his name is Jeffrey and he has something to say to you, Sire," Shelley answered.

As I looked at the man on the ground, we were joined by the members of the Inner Circle along with Mkali and her parents. Bernie motioned to Mkali and she went to stand next to her.

"Tell me what you want quickly," I commanded, "we must be on our way."

"Your Majesty, Lord Dimitri forced me to shut the people at the fortress in the dungeons and lock the gates," Jeffrey answered, "I don't know what has become of the keys."

"I'm not worried about any keys; how did he force you to do this?" I asked impatiently.

"He threatened to torture my wife and children," Jeffrey answered sadly, "but I don't know if he killed them anyway after I left to do his bidding."

"What would you have me do?"

"Please release the captives held at his camp above the palace, when I left they hadn't had anything to eat or drink for days," he begged.

"They will be released, but I need to get to the fortress now. Gustav, Stavros, have Jeffrey show you where the others are being held and release them and join me when things are secure here," I said hurriedly and moved away so I could transform.

Before shifting, I thought about the frozen wasteland and fortress from my dream and ripped open the space in front of us and I saw exactly where we needed to go. Bernie, Shelley and Mkali climbed on my back and got settled.

We'll be back! I shouted and then launched myself towards the opening. Aileene flew through the opening after me.

As we passed through the gate, Dad sent, *we'll be right behind you, after we make sure the battlefield is secure. We're sending some flying shifters with you now.*

Wu was astride a griffon and sent, *There are vast dungeons under the fortress, it will take us some time to search through each one to free the ones who are trapped there.*

All around us, I could see and feel shifters flying behind and alongside us as we made our way towards the imposing fortress, which looked more like a prison than anything else. I studied the structure as we got closer to it. The fortress had been built into the mountain so there wasn't any way to approach it from the rear. There was a semi-circular wall protecting the entrance from the front. It looked like the wall was at least fifty feet tall and was wide enough for me to land on. The wall was constructed of ice-covered stone that reflected the sunlight.

There were imposing gates guarding the entrance and they were set in a tunnel within the wall itself. The only way to enter the fortress was to enter by these gates which would normally be guarded on all sides by enemy soldiers. Since we weren't met with any violence as we approached, I assumed the entirety of Dimitri's army had gone with him. Aileene and I could fly up and over the wall, but if we wanted to bring in our people to rescue those who were trapped inside, we would have to either open the gates or destroy them. It seemed easier to me to just destroy them. The entire area smelled like death and I wasn't willing to wait much longer to get inside.

Aileene and I will take care of the gates and head inside to find my parents. Everyone else will need to locate those who are trapped in the dungeons and save them. Be careful, we don't know what surprises Dimitri may have left behind. We also don't know how many he left here to guard the castle. I will be most displeased with you if you get killed today, my comment did what I was hoping it would when I heard my people laugh.

Here's where you three get off, I sent, *while Aileene and I show you what Royal Dragons can really do when we're angry.*

Reaching out with my senses, I specifically connected with all the shifters in the fortress to see if I could figure out how many lives we were dealing with. Their life signs were in flux so it was difficult to get an accurate count but I was shocked to find that many of those within the fortress were fading fast. If we didn't hurry these shifters wouldn't survive much longer. As I sent a pulse of energy and feeling of hope through each connection, I also broadcast my thoughts, *This is Alister Rex, High King of all Theria and Slayer of Dimitri. The oppressor is dead and after today, his name will live in history as the vile usurper he was, as an example to others who may be inclined to follow in his footsteps. All his plans are in ruin. We are here to rescue you. If you stood by his side, lay down your weapons, do not fight with your rescuers, and we will remember that and will try you fairly. Oh, and if you're near the gates, you might want to stay back.*

Would you like the right or the left? I asked Aileene.

Right, my mate, Aileene answered roughly. I could feel her emotions churning within her; rage, sorrow, terror for me during my fight against Dimitri, love for the people trapped inside, love for me and hope that my parents were still alive.

I opened my emotions to Aileene as well so she could feel what I was feeling. There was great compassion in her eyes as she nuzzled my muzzle with hers before she turned to the right door.

Stand back, I sent and let loose with my flame. Royal Dragons have various levels of destructive flames at our disposal and both of us were using fire hot enough to melt rock. The doors were made of thick wood, covered and banded by iron but they were no match for our devastating flames. The opening was wide enough for us to fit through side-by-side and the entire tunnel was soon filled with the inferno of our wrath. If we had turned this flame on each other, we would have been injured but the heat from the blow back felt like a gentle caress on my scales.

We continued to bellow flame as we moved forward into the tunnel, widening the tunnel with our flame and bodies. The molten rock fell on our backs like rain and the liquid iron from the doors puddled on the ground around our feet. We doused our flames and pushed through the superheated tunnel into the courtyard. Shaking myself like a wet dog I flung the cooling rock from my back.

Aileene did the same thing as she laughed, *Promise me we can do that again some time, that was fun.*

I turned around to behold the destruction we had wrought and was amazed to see that where there had once been a tunnel, there was now a wide-open passage leading to the outside.

All clear, but it might be a bit hot when you come through the tunnel, I sent to those waiting outside the walls.

Aileen and I turned back towards the entrance to the fortress and looked for hidden enemies; we didn't find any. Casting my senses outward again I felt the same connections that were there before, unfortunately, some were even weaker now. There weren't any shifters in the courtyard and the doors leading into the fortress were shut and I presumed locked as well.

If you're inside the fortress near the front doors, stand back or you will be incinerated, I warned before Aileene and I destroyed the doors in an explosion of flames.

The rest of our party joined Aileene and me and waited to see if my instructions had changed; they hadn't.

Wu, lead the way to find every shifter in this place. Bring them to the largest room in the fortress. We'll make this our hospital. Bernie, use your healing skills on those who are nearest to death. Aileene and I will continue to work our way through this level of the fortress.

Wu rushed off and others followed him.

Can you feel your parents? Aileene asked me.

I'm not sure, but I do feel a deep well of despair coming from this way, I sent and started walking down the hallway. It was a good thing the fortress had been made for giants or there wouldn't have been enough room for me to traverse the passage in my dragon form. The air reeked of decay and we passed bodies that had been pinned to walls with steel lances. My sorrow deepened for each poor shifter displayed on the walls as a form of warning. If he wasn't already dead, I would have gladly killed Dimitri again for this travesty. Since we were connected on an emotional level, we could sense how the other was feeling and because Aileene could feel my turmoil, she sent me feelings of peace and love through our connection and I was grateful she was with me.

We stopped before a closed door and I pushed against it, but it was firmly bolted. Pushing harder, the doors gave way and we walked into the darkened room. This must have been the banquet hall but instead of tables and chairs filling the room, it was filled with the still forms of two massive dragons. I transformed and rushed over to touch my mother's body so I could put my hand on her side and lay my head on her chest. Nothing happened for what felt like an eternity but then I heard the thump-thump of her slowly beating heart. I repeated the process with my father and heard the same thing. Falling to my knees in relief, I sobbed. They were alive.

Releasing my connections with the other shifters throughout the fortress, I concentrated on connecting with the two dragons before me. Their energy was fading rapidly and they were mere moments from slipping away from me forever. Aileene went around the room and lit the logs in the fireplace and candles in their holders to bring some light into this dark place.

I found my parents, they're alive, but asleep and fading fast. We're in the banquet hall, I broadcast to everyone.

Closing my eyes I reached out and sent my thoughts towards my parents to see if they would respond, *It's me, Alister. I'm here, I've come to save you.*

Neither of them responded and I sensed their energy was draining away even quicker than it had before. I tapped into the reservoir of power inside me and began pushing energy into my parents, hoping that would give them a chance to fight whatever was killing them.

Aileene, please go find some food for them, they will be ravenous when they awake, I begged. She was behind me and leaned her head on my shoulder for a few seconds before she slipped out of the hall.

Mother, Father, I'm here, I sent again.

Alister? My father's voice sounded in my head, *are you really here or is this just a cruel dream?*

I'm here, Father, I defeated Dimitri and I'm here to save you and Mother.

*It's too late for us, son, we have lived too long with Dimitri's poison coursing through our veins. In our weakened state, we can neither shift nor move. The connection I have with your mother has frayed to the point I can barely feel it. Thank you for coming, I love you, son. You will rule Theria well—*His thoughts trailed off until his last words were barely understandable.

"No! You will not die today," I shouted and thought about what he said. There were two problems I needed to solve. First, they had poison in their bodies and it had been there since Dimitri betrayed them. The second problem was they hadn't had anything to eat or drink in all the years they lay here so they were too weak to fight for themselves. The poison had to be dealt with first or the energy I sent them would immediately drain away. The *Sanos* spell was designed to heal injuries and poison so I should be able to use that on them since I was also a Royal Dragon and could heal another of my kind. Even though both of them were dying, my mother was the weakest so I decided to try to heal her first. Laying both my hands on her side, I invoked the healing spell while tapping into my core energy.

My hands glowed brightly and I could feel the spell starting to work. My mother took a deep breath but the room started to spin because my energy was nearly depleted and I almost blacked out from the strain.

Mother, can you hear me? I sent.

Alister, I wish I could have held you one more time and tell you how much I love you, she sent and her voice faded away.

"I have to find a way to make this work," I ground out in frustration, "but I don't have the magic to create a healing spell powerful enough to nullify the poison."

I listened to the sounds of suffering throughout the fortress and heard sobbing, raised voices pleading for help and rescuers giving words of hope and encouragement to those who were trapped. It would take hours for the rest of our healers to get here, hours my parents didn't have. If I had more magic at my disposal I could heal my parents and help with the others as well.

Thinking back to my fight training with Gustav, I was reminded of the first lesson he gave about looking around to use every tool at my disposal when engaging the enemy. The poison was my enemy, my parents' weakness was my enemy and my lack of magic was my enemy. I looked around the physical space but didn't see anything that would help me. Roaring my frustration towards the ceiling, I remembered the despair I felt as Bernie lay dying on Middle Earth. At that point I didn't have a way to hold the power I needed in a land brimming with magic. This time I had a way to hold the power, but there wasn't enough magic in Theria to help me. Suddenly the answer came to me like a bolt of lightning; Middle Earth was the key!

Opening a five-foot diameter gate to Middle Earth, I felt the magic careening through the hole like a rushing river. Checking the other side of the gate to make sure there weren't any people nearby on Middle Earth, I was relieved when I only saw miles of empty, frozen tundra. Once again I tried to connect with as many shifters as possible throughout Theria but bypassed the weakest links surrounding me in the fortress. I sent a pulse of energy down each line and was staggered by the tsunami of energy that came back to me. I could feel my inner reservoir filling and expanding as the energy poured into me at least doubling in size again.

When I couldn't hold any more energy, I disconnected from the other shifters and concentrated on the connections to my parents. Pulling in magic from Middle Earth I bound that magical energy to myself and triggered the *Sanos* spell while directing the healing energy towards my parents. Closing my eyes I imagined the poison in their bodies as a dark shadow that had spread throughout most of their bodies and the healing spell was a bright light cleansing the darkness from inside them.

My parents were lying next to each other with their heads touching. Kneeling down, I placed a hand on each of their heads and poured the light from the healing spell into their bodies; my hands started to burn as the energy transferred. The magic from Middle Earth was vast like the ocean and I was trying to force that massive amount of energy through a much smaller vessel, which happened to be my body. Not only were my hands burning, but my entire body felt as though it was swelling like a rapidly expanding balloon. In my mind, I could see the light spreading throughout their bodies while the darkness slowly receded.

As the darkness of the poison fled from their bodies I transferred the stored energy from my body to theirs. I visualized this energy as a roaring flame which combined with the white light of the healing spell. Their bodies were so starved for this energy, instead of me directing it, the power was being siphoned from my reservoir at an alarming rate. The pain from this energy transfer was excruciating but I couldn't stop the magical healing until my parents were completely healed. Unfortunately, I was also powerless to stop the drain on my own energy and was unable to reach out to other shifters to get another infusion of energy from them.

It was a race to see if I could complete the healing before my reserves were depleted. The last of the darkness was chased from my parents' bodies and I managed to sever my connection to Middle Earth and close the small gate I had created. Once again, I tried to sever the connection to my parents which was draining the last of my energy but I wasn't able to. Screaming in agony my sight began to dim.

The last thing I remember was the sense of sorrow and rage coming from Aileene and her determination to return to my side before I collapsed. She didn't make it in time.

I was standing on the edge of a cliff, in my human form, and could feel the warmth of the sun at my back. The valley below was beautiful and unlike anything I had ever seen. The mountains looked to be within my grasp but were so large my mind couldn't comprehend their size. I could see people at the top of the mountain waving at me but couldn't make out their faces. They were so close, yet impossibly far away at the same time. I wanted to leap off the edge, transform into my dragon and fly to them. Somehow I knew if I did that, I would be leaving my human side behind forever. Right now, that wasn't such a bad thing. Standing there in my pain and exhaustion, I knew all that would be gone if I took to the skies.

"You could do that but think of all the people you would leave behind," a deep voice said beside me.

"But they would eventually join me, wouldn't they?" I asked.

"Yes, but you would miss the years you still have together and all the adventures you have yet to experience. Besides, Aileene asked me to make sure you came home," the voice chuckled beside me, "she's not happy with you right now, you know."

"Maybe that's enough reason to take the leap," I said.

"Oh, I doubt you really want to miss the coming years with that one, she perfectly complements you, if I do say so myself," he continued.

Glancing to my right I saw An'Ceann in his lion form. He was even bigger now and I leaned against his side for support. Immediately I was enveloped in a feeling of love and felt my energy return. When I was younger, my mom would dump laundry fresh from the dryer on me as I lay on the couch. The feeling of warmth I received from An'Ceann reminded me of that happy memory.

"So, not only do I remind you of Aslan, but I also remind you of warm laundry?" he chuckled.

"What," I laughed, "these are things that are special to me." I sobered. "Was I successful, did my efforts make a difference?"

"Let's see," An'Ceann rumbled as I leaned against him, "you helped Moss see the error of his ways and helped him and your mom forgive each other. You met Aileene and instead of rejecting her, you chose to forgive the minor thing of her almost killing you and accepted her as your mate, you defeated Dimitri's army with very few fatalities and freed the people from his oppressive rule. You brought down the barrier that separated the Kingdom of Theria from the rest of the planet and you killed the bad guy." An'Ceann flopped down on his side and carried me with him. "You showed mercy to those you didn't need to, and you chose the most difficult way to bring justice upon Dimitri to avoid possible conflict in the future. And, you nearly gave your life to save your parents. Yes, little dragon, I would say you were successful."

"Then why does part of me still want to soar off the cliff and fly towards that mountain?" I whispered.

An'Ceann's voice was filled with love and compassion as he answered me. "Because you were gravely wounded, and you witnessed the cruelty one being can bring to others. But I want you to focus on the good you have done today for those you serve and also focus on the future you have given to those who had lost hope. You are greatly loved and you love others fiercely as well. Rest with me for a while, little dragon, and know that I am proud of you."

Brimming with new purpose, I drifted off to the sound of his purring.

I squeezed the hand holding mine and heard the squeal of excitement from Aileene. She threw herself on top of me and began kissing my face.

"I could get used to this," I drawled.

Opening my eyes, I saw her narrowed, blazing, golden eyes looking down on me.

"Well, you stupid male, do not ever make me go through that again. I do not want to sit by your side, praying that you will wake up. I only have myself to blame for the first time but not for today. While you are quite formidable, you are not indestructible. Do not do this to me, ever, again," Aileene growled and punctuated each word of the last sentence by poking my chest with her finger.

"She sure told you, Stretch," Shelley snickered from his post by the door.

"I couldn't have said it better myself," Bernie agreed, "but I would have done it without the kisses."

"That's right," Shelley growled, "you better save those kisses for me."

I laughed and was grateful I didn't choose to fly off the cliff in my dream. *Thank you*, I sent to An'Ceann and I received a chuckle from him in response.

"What happened after I passed out?" I asked as Aileene helped me get out of bed and stand.

"I was returning with food for your parents when I felt you fading from our connection. I panicked a bit in my haste to be by your side," Aileene admitted.

"She burned a hole through the side of the fortress to get to you, it looks like a bomb detonated there and half the room was destroyed," Bernie teased.

"My mate was in danger, I had to get to him. You would have done the same thing in my place," Aileene huffed and I gave her a comforting hug.

"You're right, I would," Bernie said as she looked at Shelley, "I'm not criticizing, I'm just impressed with the level of destruction you wrought."

"Where are we?" I asked.

"We're still in the fortress, the fight was less than twenty-four hours ago, and your parents weren't well enough to move yet. They've been asking for you," Aileene answered.

We left the room where I awoke, and Bernie and Shelley led the way to my parents' room.

Are you really mad at me? I sent to Aileene.

Yes, but I am also very proud of you. You wouldn't be the dragon you are if you didn't put yourself in danger to save our people. However, you have to remember, you aren't alone any longer and we should face these things together. I know neither of us is ready to be married yet, but our mate bond is strong, and we complete one another in ways we don't understand yet, she replied.

You are a gift to me, Aileene, I promise to do better in the future and to remember we're a team and give each other strength. I'm nervous to meet my parents after all this time, I admitted.

We'll meet them together, Aileene sent as we entered the room where they were resting. Father was sitting in a chair next to the bed where he held Mother's hand; they both appeared to be dozing. They looked old and frail and tears immediately sprang to my eyes when I thought about what Dimitri had done to them.

"Alister," Father croaked when he saw me, and Mother tried to sit up from the bed. I hurried into the room and knelt by the bed and wept on my mother's shoulder.

"There, there, son," she soothed, "why are you crying?"

"I should have gotten to you sooner," I wept.

"We're alive because of you, and from all the stories we've been hearing, you got here as quickly as possible," she added.

"Can you even get out of bed?" I asked.

My father laughed and said, "Believe it or not, we look much better today than we did yesterday. We were drained almost to the point of death and our life force was almost depleted. When you add that to the fact we hadn't eaten in thirteen years, we were nothing but skin and bones when we transformed yesterday. Fritz and Frieda think we will make a full recovery, given enough time. We should be able to go home in a few weeks if you are able to give us daily power infusions."

"It will give us time to catch up on all we missed while we were separated. We'll also get to know our daughter as well," my mother finished as she smiled at Aileene.

Three weeks passed. I wish I could say that everything went smoothly but that wouldn't be the truth. The first difficulty we had was healing the captives we freed from the dungeons. Most of them had experienced torture of some type at the hands of Dimitri and his minions. We were able to heal most of their physical injuries, except for missing limbs, but the emotional healing from trauma would take much longer. When Dimitri was unable to kill my parents, unable to gain entrance to the Royal Palace and was trapped in Theria, he became increasingly angry at his failures and took his anger out on the people around him.

We had to examine each of the members of Dimitri's army to determine how willingly they participated in his evil. This would have been more difficult but one of those closest to Dimitri, Jeffrey, helped us determine which shifters followed Dimitri willingly. It seems that most of the members of his army were coerced in some way, but once we reunited them with their missing family members, they were willing to confess their crimes. It would take months to determine what we would do with those who were forced to follow Dimitri's evil ways.

For every joyous family reunion, there were also crushing disappointments. Wu was reunited with his children, but his wife had died when she protected another female shifter from Dimitri's wrath. Wu was devastated by this loss but was proud of his wife and the sacrifice she made to protect someone else. Those members of Dimitri's retinue who were complicit in his evil plans paid the price of their evil with their lives. None of these had family members among the captives and were still spewing hate until their mercifully quick executions.

However, our time there wasn't all filled with doom and gloom. I spent hours with my parents, giving them healing energy and telling them stories about my life on Earth. Aileene would spend that time with us as well and I was pleased to see her bonding with my parents the way she should have all along. All the members of the original Inner Circle met with my parents for hours on end as well and it was helpful to hear everyone laugh as they got reacquainted.

Shelley told me I had to come up with a way to differentiate my parents, Phillip and Beatrice from my parents, Albert and Fiona, because it was too confusing for him. He suggested Ma and Pa for Phillip and Beatrice but my father gave him a look only a Royal Dragon can give so Shelley dropped that idea. I would continue to call Albert and Fiona mom and dad and call Phillip and Beatrice Father and Mother.

Aileene, Bernie, Shelley and I spent the evenings together after dinner and I was pleased to see the three of them building the friendship they were always meant to have.

When we weren't together Aileene and Bernie would work with Mkali on her squire training and Mkali was included at our dinner table and when we would hang out together. Even though she was younger than us, we all liked having her around and I was frequently amazed at her maturity and fierce commitment to serving as one of my Knights one day.

We left the fortress after three weeks and my parents looked the way I remembered them from my childhood. We explored the fortress before we left and took anything we thought we might need in the future. I had decided the only way to cleanse the evil from that place was to melt it into the ground. We sent the others ahead as we hovered in the air and each of us took a side of the fortress to destroy. Once we were in place, I gave the signal and we let loose with our fire. The resulting heat, destruction and explosions were spectacular and after about fifteen minutes there wasn't anything left of the fortress but a puddle of cooling lava.

Aileen and I led the procession to the gate I left open when we flew through it to free the people in Dimitri's fortress. Our friends and the refugees we were bringing back to the Royal Palace came next and my parents brought up the rear. As soon as Aileene and I passed through the gate, we landed and transformed and stood side by side until my parents also flew through the opening. Once everyone had come through, I closed the gate with a thought and also closed the chapter on Dimitri and his reign of terror.

Are you going to take down the shield surrounding the palace? I sent to my dad, Phillip.

I could hear the humor in his thoughts as he answered, *No, son, that's your job. You're the King, only you have the power to take it down.*

But I thought you and Mother would take your thrones again, I sent, surprise evident in my sending.

No, once we get everything back in order, your father and I are planning on taking a nice, long vacation, Mother sent to me.

How long? I wondered.

Probably only six months or so, she sent and then transformed into her human form and laughed at the expression on my face.

She walked up to me and placed her hand on my cheek. "I'm so proud of you son and everything you have accomplished so far. You are a great King and I know Aileene will make an amazing Queen when it's her time."

"That might still take a while," Aileene answered, "I don't have him trained the way I want him yet." She smiled sweetly and grabbed my hand.

All my parents laughed at my stunned expression and then everybody else joined in. It sounded so good to hear everyone laughing, I didn't mind that they were laughing at me. I transformed my teeth so they were pointed, dragon teeth and bit my hand to draw some blood. Aileene and I walked up to the barrier, I placed my bloody hand on the shield and with a flash of bright light it winked out of existence. We were home, and I was excited to see what our next adventure would be.

EPILOGUE

From my vantage point on the cliff I looked down at a valley filled with six armies. There were shifters of every description arrayed against one another under six different battle flags: the Eutherian flag, a golden drake on a field of red, the Metatherian flag, a snarling golden jaguar on a field of black, the Sirenean flag, a red Long Dragon on a field of yellow, the Carnivorian flag, a brown lion on an orange background, the Marsupian flag, a Mallorn tree with silver bark and golden leaves on a blue background and the Cetacean flag, a green mermaid on a purple background.

I watched in horror as the armies met in the middle and began to decimate one another. As the last shifter fell, I saw myself in dragon form flying with Aileene towards the carnage. The bodies of Shelley, Bernie, Mkali and the rest of my friends were lying among the other shifters on the field of battle. I fell to my knees and wept as I heard the keening wails coming from Aileene and me in our dragon forms.

I felt a paw on my shoulder and knew An'Ceann was standing behind me. He spoke to me, his voice hoarse with emotion. "All your people across the planet need you; they need you to reunite them under one banner. They need the High King."

The End

AFTERWORD

Thank you for reading *Return* and especially for reading all the way to the end. I hope you enjoyed the book enough to write a review on Amazon. Independent authors need reviews to get noticed.

It's fun to write about Alister, Bernie, Shelley and now Aileene, and to see how they are developing as characters. Someone asked me if I put part of myself in Alister and I answered, "I hope so." Alister faces many difficult challenges but realizes how fortunate he is to have a great support system of people who love him. Because of them, he can do more than he thinks is possible.

Part of my inspiration comes from when I was a boy and read The Hardy Boys books. I always loved the friendships Joe and Frank Hardy had, and how well they were written. They were only able to solve the mysteries they did because of the support they received from friends and family. So many great stories have been written over the years with supportive friends who helped the main character succeed. (Frodo wouldn't have been able to destroy the ring without Sam.) I hope you have good friends who support you and experience life's adventures with you.

The next book is *Reunite, Dragonborn Book Three* and I really look forward to sharing that story with you as well. I plan to publish

Reunite this year, but the release date will depend on how many people read *Return* and leave reviews.

I would love to know your favorite scenes in my books and hear about parents reading these books to their kids. My email address is bretthumphreyauthor@gmail.com. You can also reach me on my website. Visit www.bretthumphreyauthor.com for cool stuff and updates on what's next in this series, and beyond.

I hope Alister and his friends inspire you to make a positive impact in the life of someone you connect with every day.

Brett Humphrey
February 2020

Protect the Weak!

Made in the USA
Columbia, SC
25 April 2022